LOVING SANC

Slick Rock 12

Becca Van

MENAGE EVERLASTING

Siren Publishing, Inc.
www.SirenPublishing.com

A SIREN PUBLISHING BOOK
IMPRINT: Ménage Everlasting

LOVING SANCTUARY
Copyright © 2015 by Becca Van

ISBN: 978-1-63259-059-6

First Printing: February 2015

Cover design by Les Byerley
All art and logo copyright © 2015 by Siren Publishing, Inc.

Printed in the U.S.A.

PUBLISHER
Siren Publishing, Inc.
www.SirenPublishing.com

LOVING SANCTUARY

Slick Rock 12

BECCA VAN
Copyright © 2015

Prologue

Fort Collins, two weeks previously

Sabrina Monroe stood at the slightly ajar door to her boss's office, and her heart stuttered when she heard his voice.

"I don't give a fuck how you do it, just make sure that bitch dies and soon. If Sabrina goes to the cops, I'm ruined. I will make damn sure that I take you down with me if you don't silence that slut."

Sabrina's heart flipped in her chest, and the air felt like it had backed up in her lungs. She wanted to turn around and run away, but she couldn't get her feet to obey her command. She should be turning on her heal and leaving, but she felt frozen, her mind disconnected from her body. She should have left as soon as she accidentally opened that e-mail and read it just before she left work over two hours ago.

She'd left her cell phone in the drawer of her desk and had felt lost without it, so instead of waiting to get it the next day at work she'd come back to the office after hours. She hadn't expected her boss to still be there. She'd thought she would have the place all to herself. Her heart pounded and she couldn't breathe properly, but finally she got her feet to obey her brain and she turned around, snatched her cell from her desk drawer, and took off.

She knew she was in big trouble after having heard him on the phone. She knew that he was telling whoever was on the other end of the line to kill her. She hadn't been sure that Harvey had noticed her opening and reading that e-mail, but after hearing what he'd just said, her suspicions were confirmed. She'd always thought that Harvey was a shady character, because he always seemed so secretive. But she'd never had any proof that he was up to no good, that was until this afternoon and that dreaded e-mail. She'd often wondered what he was up to when he scheduled meetings after hours. Most people dealt with business during office hours and didn't wait until the offices were empty to meet with clients. But again she'd had no proof of who he met or what he was doing.

God knew who he'd been talking to, but it didn't really matter. Her life was in danger and she needed to run. To hide.

Sabrina wished she could go to the police station, but other than reading that e-mail, which she hadn't thought to copy, she had no evidence of what her boss was doing. It would be her word against his, and since he was the owner of the large computer-and-software-manufacturing firm, she couldn't see anyone believing her. She had to leave town. There was no time to go back to her shared apartment because when he found out she was missing from her office tomorrow, she had no doubt he would send whomever he was talking to after her. That was if the goon wasn't already after her. For all she knew he could already be on his way to her home.

Oh, God. She had probably put her roommate Nicole in danger. She would have to contact her before she left town. There was no way she could tell Nic what was going on. If her friend knew and her boss did send someone after Sab, she would be in peril, too. No. It would be better to keep her mouth shut. Hopefully Nicole would be safe since she didn't know anything.

Thank God she always carried all her ID, credit cards, and bank details with her. It didn't matter that she was leaving material things behind. Nothing mattered but escaping and surviving. If Harvey Noble or his hirelings caught up with her, she couldn't see any of them letting her live. She knew too much. Harvey had said her name after he'd ordered his goon to find her and kill her. She felt sick with fear but couldn't stop. She had to move and fast.

Sabrina hurried down the street and looked about wildly, her heartbeat pounding in her chest every time someone even looked at her. She practically ran all the way to the bank, and after withdrawing as much as her daily limit allowed, she raced away. She stopped in the street and tried to think clearly, but that was damn hard when she was so scared. She looked about her again and nearly sagged with relief when she realized no one was taking any notice of her.

Without consciously thinking about what she was doing, she opened her cell phone and removed the battery and then dumped it into a trash can. She started walking again without a destination in mind, and after she'd traveled another block she deliberately dropped her cell onto the sidewalk and was pleased when it shattered into several pieces and then dumped it into another trash can. Again she hurried forward, not caring where she was going but acutely aware of every person close-by.

When she saw the pay phone, she walked over to it and picked up the receiver and dialed.

"Hello." Nicole's familiar voice brought tears to her eyes, and she took a deep breath and swallowed around the lump in her throat.

"Nic, it's me," Sab said.

"Sabrina? Where are you? Are you okay? You sound funny."

"Um, I just got some bad news. I have to leave and I don't know if I'll be able to return. A family member died and I have to leave the state."

"But you don't have any fam..."

"Sublet my room out and sell anything of my things you like, or keep it if that's what you want."

"Sabrina?"

"I have to go. Take care, Nicole." Sabrina swiped at the tears streaming down her face. She'd heard the bewilderment and worry in her friend's voice, but it was better that she knew nothing. She couldn't be hurt if she didn't know what was going on.

Could she?

Please, God, keep Nicole safe.

Sabrina replaced the handset on the hook and then started walking again, her mind in a whirl as she tried to figure out what to do next.

She was only vaguely aware of the bus that passed her and then stopped as it pulled into the terminal. She glanced at the buses lined up awaiting their passengers and stopped in her tracks. She retraced her steps and, after making sure no one was watching her car, got into it and drove it to the nearest used car lot. She was just in time because the guy was starting to close up.

Sabrina didn't get anywhere near what the car was worth, but when she walked out of the guy's office she had another thousand dollars in her purse.

Should she take the chance and go to the police before she left town, or should she just get out of town and worry about contacting the police later? She watched TV and heard how witnesses had been killed even while in protective custody. Could she really put her life into someone else's hands?

No. Run.

She got onto the next bus out of Fort Collins.

Chapter One

Present Day

Sabrina Brown glanced behind her as she hurried down the street of the small rural Colorado town of Slick Rock. Her heart was racing, and she was so scared she was shaking and having trouble staying on her feet.

She'd been running for the last two weeks, but no matter where she ended up she always felt like someone was watching her, following her. Whenever she'd looked, she'd never seen anyone taking any notice of her, and although she felt like she was getting paranoid, she couldn't seem to help it. Her imagination hadn't let up since that fateful afternoon two weeks ago. She was tired, hungry, and scared, plus she didn't feel very well, and didn't think she'd ever feel safe again. Being on the move was taking everything out of her. She was going through what little money she had left, because she'd been too afraid to use any of her credit cards. If she did that, then he and whoever he'd threatened on the phone to kill her would be on to her.

Will I ever be safe again? Will I ever be able to stop and smell the roses?

Sabrina couldn't see that happening anytime soon. She was in a panic because she thought she'd seen someone watching her. Her chest was aching, and her hand was wrapped tight around the handle of her purse, and she was gasping for breath as she hurried along the street.

She'd started in her hometown of Fort Collins and had spent the last two weeks going from bus to bus, from one place to another, doubling back and then moving forward again. The bus had arrived at Slick Rock fifteen minutes ago, and there wasn't another one leaving town for a week. She'd catnapped over the last two weeks but hadn't really slept deeply, and when she had slept, it was no more than an hour or two. She was totally exhausted and so hungry. She'd managed to buy a heap of granola bars, but food had taken a backseat to her terror, and now she was paying for that. She was often lightheaded and wondered if one day soon she would pass out and just not wake up. She forced that defeatist, morbid thought aside as she continued on.

Sabrina cursed her stupidity. She hadn't even asked the driver when she got on the last bus where it was going because she hadn't really cared. As long as it was away from Fort Collins, that was all that mattered. But now she was stuck and she had no idea what she was going to do. The next bus out of town wasn't due to leave Slick Rock for another week, and the one she'd arrived on was already gone.

She wasn't sure how long her money was going to last. Especially since she was now going to have to find accommodation of some sort. She was so damn hungry her stomach was in constant pain and it felt like her stomach was pressing against her spine, so she decided to take the chance to stop for something to eat and a cup of coffee.

Sabrina checked the road and, after making sure it was clear, crossed it. The moment she entered the diner she felt every eye turn her way. It was a disconcerting feeling to be the center of attention, and even though she understood it—a stranger in a small rural town— she didn't like it. After a cursory glance around the room and finding numerous eyes on her, she lowered her head and hurried to an empty stool at the counter.

Is it my imagination or has the conversation stopped?

The waitress came over, and she put the rest of the patrons from her mind. "What'll you have, honey?"

"Coffee, black please, and some apple pie and ice cream." Sabby didn't usually start with dessert, but she figured the sugar would help circumvent the lightheadedness she'd been feeling. If she was still hungry after her pie, then she would order a decent meal.

She glanced at the board on the wall, noting all the food and the specials, and her mouth began to water. When her vision wavered and perspiration formed on her brow, she clutched at the edge of the counter and inhaled deeply. The last thing she needed was to draw more attention to herself if she passed out.

"Here you go, honey," the waitress said as she put the mug and plate in front of her. "Enjoy."

"Thanks." Sab picked up the spoon, unwrapped the napkin from around it, and dug in. She nearly moaned as the sweetness exploded on her tongue, but she held it in. She closed her eyes instead and savored the wonderful taste of apples, cinnamon, and pastry. She savored each and every bite and then scraped the remaining crumbs and melted ice cream up until there was nothing left. Now that her hunger was slightly appeased, she picked up her coffee and sipped it while perusing the menu.

She tried to calculate how much money she had left in her mind, but after buying so many bus tickets she didn't have a clue. And although she wanted to pull her wallet out to count it out, she wasn't about to do that in front of prying eyes.

The waitress came back over. "Do you want more coffee and pie?"

Sabrina would love more pie, but until she'd figured out her finances she wasn't going to indulge. "Just the coffee, please."

"You're not from around here, are you?" the waitress asked as she refilled Sab's mug.

"No."

"Did you come in on the bus?"

"Yes."

"So you're staying for a while," the waitress said. "Have you got a place to stay yet?"

"No. Can you recommend somewhere?"

"There's the Slick Rock Hotel just down the street, or the motel to the north."

"Can you tell me which one is cheaper?" Sab almost whispered her question so that no one else would hear.

"That would be the hotel, honey."

"Okay, thank you." Sab finished her coffee and left some money on the counter to cover her bill and a small tip. She slid off the stool, and as she turned the dizziness returned with a vengeance. Sweat popped out on her brow and her body began to ache, but what worried her the most was that her vision had dimmed and she couldn't see a thing. She grabbed for the closest thing, which was the stool, and although she felt herself falling she couldn't do a thing to stop it. She braced herself as best she could with her weak limbs, trying to prepare for the impact with the floor, but she never hit.

Strong arms scooped her up, and then she was being cradled against a warm, muscular body. She wanted to open her eyes to see who held her, but she couldn't. Her whole body was sensitive with pain, and she just didn't have the energy. Sabrina whimpered as the sweat began to run down her face and formed all over her skin, and even though she must be hot, she felt so cold.

"Shh, it's all right, sweetheart. Just rest. We'll take care of you."

Sabrina sighed and then let her body go lax as she drifted to sleep.

* * * *

Trick Wendall had just entered the diner to meet his brothers, Trent and Tristan, for lunch. He'd noticed the young woman at the counter through the window and had been speculating about who she was as he searched the interior for his brothers. Just before he'd come level with her stool, she'd slid from it and then swayed on her feet.

She'd reached out to grip the stool, but that hadn't been enough to stop her fall. He was glad that he had quick reflexes and was able to scoop her up into his arms before she hit the linoleum floor.

She stiffened in his arms as if afraid, and the whimper that left her mouth went straight to his heart. She was a sweet bundle in his arms and she smelled so fresh and clean, but when he saw the perspiration on her brow and felt her shiver before she went limp in his hold, he realized she was sick.

"Someone call the doc," Trick called out.

"Done," Hilda, the middle-aged owner and waitress, said as she hung up the phone. "He'll be here in a moment. Why don't you bring her to the office so he can check her over in privacy?"

"Do you need some help, bro?" Trent asked when he and Tristan stopped in front of him.

Trick nodded. "One of you go hold the door to the back open."

Tristan and Trent rushed ahead of him as Trick carried the woman around the counter to the side door leading to the back.

"What do you think's wrong with her?" Tristan asked.

"I don't know," Trick answered. "Could be the flu. It's been making the rounds."

"She's tiny," Trent said as Trick walked passed him. "She doesn't look like she weighs much."

"No." Trick sighed as he looked down at the woman's beautiful face. Some of her blonde hair had come loose from her ponytail and brushed over his skin. Her lips were full but pale, a testament to her being ill. She was a stunning woman, and he wondered if her eyes were blue. He shuffled past Tristan as he held Hilda's office door open and headed straight for the sofa against the wall.

"Put that cushion at the end of the sofa and grab that throw rug," Trick said to Trent and waited until his brother did so, before he carefully placed her on the couch. He took the throw from Trent and covered her with it.

"Help me get her shoes off," he said, and then he moved toward her feet. He wrapped his hand around her ankle and couldn't help but notice how petite she was. Her feet were so small that his hand looked big and clumsy. He removed her shoe and dropped it on the floor as Tristan did the other.

"She's so damn tiny," Trent whispered as he squatted down near her head and placed the palm of his hand over her brow. "Shit! She's got a fever."

"Move aside and let me check her out," the doc said as he entered the room.

Trick and his brothers watched as the doctor placed the electronic thermometer in her ear. Then he felt up and down her neck, checked the response of her eyes with a pen light, and took her blood pressure. Trick had been right. Her eyes were a beautiful sky blue.

"She's got the flu, and from the looks of her, she hasn't been taking care of herself. She needs to rest, and when the fever has passed she'll need food. I don't think she's been eating properly. Her face looks a little gaunt, as if she's recently lost weight and she has dark smudges under her eyes, which tells me she's not sleeping. Plus there's the fact that her clothes look a little loose."

"I brought her purse," Hilda said as she entered the room. "I also called Luke to let him know what's going on. He and Damon will be here in a minute."

Trick took the purse from Hilda and nodded his thanks. He wanted to open that purse and find out who she was, but he didn't. He'd leave that to the law.

"Search her purse," the doc said.

"Shouldn't I wait until Luke and Damon get here?"

"No. I want to know if she's allergic to anything or has a medical condition."

Trick opened the purse and tipped out the contents. There wasn't much inside. A box of tampons, a brush, a small bottle of perfume, and a wallet. He turned to Hilda. "Did she tell you who she is?"

"No. Just that she came in on the bus," Hilda said.

"She didn't have another bag with her?" Trent asked.

"Not that I know of."

"She could have left it at the bus station instead of lugging it around town," Tristan suggested.

"I'll send someone to check," Hilda said before leaving again.

Trick opened the wallet and looked at her license through the plastic. "Her name is Sabrina Brown and she lives in Fort Collins."

Sheriffs Luke Sun-Walker and Damon Osborne entered the office. Trick handed Sabrina's wallet over when Luke wiggled his fingers at him. "I'll check her out. She might be on the run from the law."

"I don't think that's the case." Tristan stepped closer to Sabrina and stared at Luke with his hands on his hips. Trick felt protective of Sabrina, and when he glanced over at Trent he saw that his younger brother felt the same.

He had been drawn to her before he'd even seen her face, and now that he had, he wanted to get to know her and hopefully have a relationship with her, but first he and his brothers needed to take care of her so she could recover from her illness.

"I need to check, Tristan. With all the shit that has gone down around here lately, with the danger following the women who come to this town, we need to be prepared."

"And what if she is on the run? Are you going to lock her up?" Trent asked as he moved to stand between Sabrina and the Sheriff.

"If I have to."

"Damn it, Luke." Trent shoved his fingers through his hair and sighed.

"It's my job. I don't interfere in with your construction business, so you stay out of mine. Got it?"

"Calm down," Trick said. "Luke needs to do his job, guys."

"Fine. Sorry," Trent said before extending his hand to Luke.

"No problem." Luke shook his and then Tristan's hand. "Are you three going to take care of her, or do you want me to make other arrangements?"

"No, we'll look after her," Trick said.

"I'll let you know what I find out," Luke said before taking note of Sabrina's details, and then he left.

"Call if you need anything," Damon said before he followed Luke out.

Hilda came back carrying a small backpack.

"That's it?" Trick asked.

Hilda nodded. "She has two changes of clothes."

"Nothing else?" Trent asked.

Hilda shook her head.

"Shit." Trick sighed and took the bag from Hilda. He opened Sabrina's wallet to find a thousand dollars in cash, a credit card, and an ATM card. There was nothing else besides her license. "She's definitely on the run." Trick looked at his brothers.

"Yeah," Trent said. "But why?"

Chapter Two

Trent drove the truck toward home, but he continually glanced in the rearview mirror at Trick. His brother was in the backseat and had Sabrina's head in his lap. Tristan was sitting in the front passenger seat, but he was half turned and watching Sabrina, too.

The doc had told them to keep her fluids up as she fought the effects of the flu, and he was going to make sure that she drank often. He was glad that he and Tristan had just finished renovating an old house on the outskirts of town and had been planning to take a couple of weeks' break now that the weather was getting colder. Their construction business was booming, and he and Tris had been so busy with all the new houses going up, plus renovations, they'd barely had time to scratch themselves. He was looking forward to some downtime, especially now that they had Sabrina to look after.

They had even helped out their older brother Trick by refurbishing the new maternity and baby store for him and his new business partner, Tori.

Trent smiled as he remembered how enthusiastic his older hard-ass brother had been about starting up a new business. At first he'd thought that Trick was attracted to Tori, and even though she was a fine-looking woman, beautiful and sexy, Trent hadn't felt a connection to her.

Tristan must have thought the same thing, because after meeting Tori one night at the Slick Rock Hotel, and after she was gone, he had asked Trick outright if he was attracted to her. Trick had denied it, but he'd had a smile on his face, so Trent had started questioning him, too. Their older brother had finally come clean and told them that he was trying to rile up the Katz brothers since they had made it blatantly obvious that they had thought of the beautiful woman as theirs. It had worked, too, and Tori had been pissed off at Luther's, Jeremiah's, and Bryant's displays of possession.

But things had worked out for them in the end, and now they were all involved in a loving ménage relationship. Trent and his brothers wanted that, too, but there were so few women in the small rural town, and whenever anyone new came along, they were snapped up as fast as he could blink. None of them were getting any younger, and he felt as if time was slipping by, and so were their chances of finding that special woman to settle down with.

"She okay?" Trent glanced in the mirror again, cursing the fact that he couldn't see Sabrina.

"She's still hot," Trick answered as he met his gaze. "And she keeps shivering."

Trent nodded and looked back to the road. He hated that she was sick, but other than try to keep her comfortable there wasn't much they could do.

His mind drifted as he drove.

He and Tristan were thirty-three years old, and he was sick and tired of having meaningless sex. Not that he hooked up with the opposite sex often, but he wanted something permanent like all the others had. Thirty-five-year-old Trick had been more antsy than usual, too. He'd been snapping and snarling at them, but when he or Tristan had tried to get their older-by-two-years brother to talk with them, he'd just shrugged his shoulders and clammed up tight. But Trent had a feeling Trick was pining for a woman they could all share, too. He and Tristan had seen him watching the other ménage trios and quartets with envy in his eyes.

Trick had had to grow up young and take on a huge responsibility after their parents had died years before in a car accident while they had been away on holiday, and Trent had begun to wonder if his older brother would ever let his guard down and let a woman in to see that he could be a loving, tender man, but he couldn't see that happening anytime soon. Trick had had to take on the responsibility of the bank, and he'd spent a lot of time learning the ropes just after he'd turned twenty.

Neither he nor Tristan had ever been interested in working in the bank, and although none of them needed to work since they were well off, he and his twin brother loved working in the construction industry. He loved the smell of freshly cut wood and seeing things come together to form cupboards, buildings, and such, knowing he'd help build them with his own hands. He and Tris would probably go mad if they had to spend all their working hours behind a desk in an office. He loved working outside and wouldn't change his job for a million bucks.

"How is she?" Trent asked as he glanced in the mirror again.

"Still sleeping," Trick answered. "And she's shivering because of the fever."

"We'll be home in a minute," Tris said. "We can get her into a bed and warmed up real soon."

Trent slowed the truck and turned onto their road, and moments later he parked close to the front porch. Tristan was out before he'd even taken his seat belt off and was opening the back door for Trick.

"Do you want me to carry her?" Tristan asked as Trent walked around the truck to join them.

"No, I've got her. Just open up so we can put her to bed. She's going to need lots of rest."

Trent unlocked and opened the front door then stood aside so Trick could enter. He followed his brother as he walked down the hall toward the master bedroom, and his heart flipped in his chest. They had more than one guest room Trick could have put Sabrina in, and he knew his brother's actions spoke volumes. The master bedroom had been set up a couple of years ago, and no one had entered it except to dust and vacuum. None of them had brought a woman home, preferring to slake their lust with consensual females elsewhere, but it had been an unspoken agreement between the three of them that this room would remain unoccupied until they had found the woman they wanted to spend the rest of their lives with. It was damn significant that his brother had brought her to this room.

Trent rushed to the bed and pulled the covers down. "Should we take her clothes off?"

Trick gently placed Sabrina on the bed. "I'm not sure. What do you guys think?"

Tristan moved closer to the bed and stared down at the small woman. "I think we should. She's sweating and shivering. I don't think she'll be too comfortable sleeping in clothes. We can leave her underwear on and she can sleep in one of our T-shirts."

Trent hurried away to get one of his shirts, and when he came back, his brothers had already managed to remove her sweater and shirt, and were working on her jeans. His breath caught in his throat when he saw her full breasts spilling over the top of her lacy bra, and if he stared hard enough, he could just make out her pinky-brown areolae and her nipples. When he realized what he was doing, he felt like a real bastard. The poor woman was asleep, sick, and couldn't even cover herself. He averted his eyes from her chest and helped pull the shirt over her head.

"Remove her bra," Trick said as he gently lifted Sabrina up and against his chest. Trent pushed his hands under the shirt and nearly moaned when they connected with the hot silkiness of her skin, but he pushed his lascivious thoughts aside, unhooked her bra, pulled the T-shirt back down, and then searched up her arms to her shoulders to remove the straps from her arms. When he'd pulled them off, he once more pushed up under the shirt, but this time at the front, and tugged the garment from beneath it.

Trick laid her back down onto the bed and pulled the covers up to her shoulders. Trent sat on the side of the bed and stroked the loose tendrils of blonde hair away from her face. He hated feeling the heat radiating from her skin and decided to get a cold washcloth to wash her face with. He rose to his feet and went into the large en suite bathroom, and then he gently rubbed the cool cloth over her face.

She sighed and then mumbled incoherently, but Trent couldn't work out what she said. One of her arms flailed, and her little hand connected with his chest. Trick kneeled on the other side of the bed and placed his hand on her forehead and then shifted it to her neck where he hadn't wiped the cool cloth yet.

"Her temperature is spiking again," Trent said, and frowned. "We need to get her cooled down. Tristan, go run a tepid bath."

Tristan hurried to the bathroom, and Trent heard the water come on. "Should we call the doc again?"

"Not yet. Let's see if we can get her fever down first. She needs to drink, too." Trick moved toward the bedroom door. "I'll go and get a jug of water and a glass. I want to see if we can get some fluids into her before we try and bring her temperature down."

Trent dropped the cloth onto the floor and moved Sabrina until her back was resting against his front. They needed her sitting up so she could drink without choking. It wasn't long before Trick was back, and he slowly fed her water. At first Sabrina had turned her head away when his brother had placed the glass against her lips, but Trick was determined, so he'd taken hold of her chin in his hand and then slowly trickled the water into her mouth. She must have been thirsty, because as the water first dripped into her mouth she'd relaxed instead of trying to fight them and tried to gulp it down. Trick hadn't let her of course, because none of them wanted her throwing up. His brother had been resolute about giving her the thirst-quenching water a little at a time until half the glass was gone.

"All right." Trick placed the glass on the bedside table. "Let's get her in the bath."

Trent shifted her in his arms and carried her to the bathroom. Between the three of them, they removed her clothes and then Trick took his off. Trent handed her over, and then Trick stepped into the cool water. "Damn, that's fucking cold. Get ready to help me to restrain her. She's so hot and the tepid water is going to make her fight."

"I'll change places with you if you want," Tristan said as he ran his eyes all over Sabrina's body. "I feel the need to cool off."

"You're not the only one," Trent said and adjusted the fit of his jeans. "I'm so fucking hot and hard right now."

"Cut it out," Trick snapped. "This isn't the time."

"Like you haven't noticed how damn beautiful and sexy she is." Tristan snickered as he looked toward Trick's burgeoning erection. "It's kind of hard to miss, bro."

Trick sucked in a breath as he sank into the water and immediately wrapped his arms around Sabrina's arms and chest, and hooked his legs around hers when she started thrashing and yelling. When Trent picked up some of the words, his heart felt like it froze in his chest.

"No. Don't…want…die. Run…" Her blue eyes were wide open but glazed over with fever, and she didn't look comprehending at all. After a while, she quieted in Trick's arms, her panted breaths slowed, and her eyes drifted shut.

Trick stood up, handed her over to him and Tristan, and then got out of the tub. He and Tris dried her off, pulled the shirt back on, and then Tristan carried her back to the bed and covered her up. She sighed as she snuggled into the pillow, and Trent was pleased to see that she seemed to be resting more peacefully than before.

Trick came out fully dressed and, after nodding to the door, left for the kitchen. Trent didn't want to leave her, but he and his brothers had a lot to discuss and they needed to contact Luke. They needed to find out everything they could about Sabrina Brown and as quickly as possible.

Trick was already on his cell when he entered the kitchen, and he didn't need to ask who his brother was talking to.

"So you found nothing?" Trick frowned and then sighed as he ran his fingers through his hair. "Damn. Okay, we'll have to talk to her when she's better." He paused to listen. "Yeah, I'll let you know as soon as I find out anything. Thanks, Luke."

"She's not on the run from the law, is she?" Trent stated more than asked.

"No."

"Then who the hell is she running from?"

Trick shrugged. "How the hell am I supposed to know? You know damn well that we haven't been able to talk to her yet."

"Yeah, I know." Trent scrubbed a hand down his face with frustration.

"We need to protect her," Tristan said as he looked toward the doorway. "She's such a little thing. We can't let anyone hurt her."

"No," Trick said.

Then Tristan decided to ask the question that had been circling around in his mind from the moment he'd seen Sabrina, and had been on the tip of his tongue when Trick had carried her into the master bedroom. "She's the one, isn't she?"

"She could be," Trick replied. "But don't you two go pushing her. We don't want her running away. You could fuck everything up if you get impatient."

Trent knew he was right. He and Tristan were always impatient, because when they saw something they wanted, nothing stopped them from getting it. But this time was different. He'd never been instantly attracted to a woman before, not like he was with Sabrina, nor had his brothers. Of course they'd been drawn to other women and had enticed them into their beds with those women's consent, before making sure they knew it wasn't permanent and was just for a good time. But this was way more than that. It was so different to anything he'd experienced before. They'd never taken a stranger in because she was sick or hurt. Although needless to say, they had stopped to help if women needed assistance because they didn't like seeing any woman or child in trouble.

The need to nurture and hold Sabrina was a yearning deep in his heart and soul. One he'd never harbored before. However, the need to protect her was a craving deep in his gut, almost like a living entity, and one he wasn't about to ignore.

The stunning woman in their master bedroom was all of his hopes and dreams, and he wasn't about to let her go, not if he could help it. And from the resolute look on Tristan's face, he felt the same way. Hopefully, when Sabrina had recovered from the flu, they could talk her into staying with them.

From what they'd heard her mutter, that wasn't going to be easy. She was going to be wary, and it was going to take time to gain her trust. He wanted to know who she was running from and why, and he and his brothers, plus the rest of the men in this town, would gather and watch and wait. Trent, Tristan, and Trick would be there to stand in front of her if necessary, and if everything else went to plan they would stand at her sides for the rest of their lives.

Trent was brought out of his introspection when Tris nudged his elbow and handed him a beer. He took a sip and then glanced over at Trick. His older brother was glancing from him to Tris and back again.

"Did you hear me?" Trick asked.

"Yeah, I heard. Don't worry, I know how important this is," Trent said.

"So do I." Tristan leaned against the kitchen counter and swigged at his beer. "Did Luke have any information on her?"

"Other than what we got off of her driver's license, no."

"What about family?" Trent asked. "Did he find any?"

"No. She's alone," Trick replied.

"Damn." Trent sighed. "That must be hard. She's only twenty-four."

Trick and Tristan both nodded.

"Luke was going to see if he could get a phone number for the address on her license and call it. He was worried that she could be running from a man."

"Fuck!" Trent wanted to slam his beer bottle onto the counter with frustration, but he didn't. He placed it down gently before meeting Trick's gaze again. "I hadn't even thought about her having a man in her life. Jesus, I don't even want to think about her being kissed, touched by—"

"Stop it, Trent," Trick snapped. "You're getting too far ahead. We don't know anything about this woman, and until we do she's off limits. Understand?"

"No, I don't understand." Trent stepped closer to Trick and got in his face. "She's not married or engaged. There are no rings on her fingers."

Tristan stepped between them and shoved them apart. "Calm the hell down, Trent. You know as well as I do that means nothing in this day and age. Trick's right. Until we know more she's off limits."

"When did you decide to align yourself with Mr. Hard-ass?"

"Shit, Trent. Stop thinking with your dick," Tristan said.

"My dick has nothing to do with it." Trent moved around the counter and sat on a stool. "Well, maybe a little, but not all."

Tristan snorted and smiled, and then all three of them were laughing. They had always been like that. Snapping and snarling at each other until someone said something to break the ice and then they laughed to ease the tension.

If anyone saw them they'd probably think they were nuts.

Trent couldn't wait to see what Sabrina thought.

Chapter Three

She groaned as she slowly began to wake, her hand sliding across cool cotton as if searching for something. "Why do I feel so bad?" she muttered.

Sabrina felt like shit. Her body was achy, she had a headache, and her nose and her eyes were starting to run. When she opened her eyes and looked around, she found herself in a strange bedroom and bed. She shifted and realized that she wasn't wearing her clothes anymore and wondered what had happened. Her brow scrunched as she frowned and tried to remember how she'd gotten to wherever she was.

The last thing she remembered was eating apple pie and drinking coffee at the diner. After that everything was blank. She hadn't felt well but had put it down to not eating or sleeping, but from the way she was feeling, she guessed she'd been wrong.

She caught the sound of men's voices and decided it was time to find out what the hell was going on. When she flung the covers aside and saw the large T-shirt covering her body, she gasped. She only had her panties on besides the shirt. Had they seen her nearly naked body? Heat suffused her cheeks, but she pushed her embarrassment aside. Maybe whoever had removed her clothes had done it to make her more comfortable. She was thankful because there was nothing worse than sleeping in her clothes as far as she was concerned.

Her head swam for a moment as she pushed to her feet, and she sighed with relief when it settled again. She headed to the door on the other side of the bed and gasped with awe when she saw the massive bathroom. It was so damn big she could nearly have had a party in it.

The shower was huge with multiple shower heads, and the spa bath was big enough for about six people. There were three sinks in the vanity, and a mirror took up the whole wall above it. It was beautiful, and she could just see herself relaxing in that bath, soaking her aches and pains away.

Sab walked to the door near the shower and was pleased to find a toilet enclosed. After using the facilities and washing her hands she found a new toothbrush. She quickly brushed her teeth and then decided to go find whoever owned the house, and find out where she was. But first she needed to cover up. When she saw her clothes on the small sofa against the far wall, she walked over to them and pulled her sweater and jeans on. There was no way she was confronting anyone without a bit of armor in place. She'd never been comfortable showing her wares to anyone, and she wasn't about to do it now.

The timber floor was cool under her bare feet, and she took in her surroundings as she walked slowly toward the voices. There were four bedrooms, and she noticed that they were neat and tidy. The last bedroom she passed had a few clothes draped over the dresser, but there was nothing on the floor and the bed was made like the other two.

The living room was huge. The furniture was large with a navy-blue leather sofa and reclining armchairs off to either side. A chunky wooden coffee table sat over a colorful navy-and-green rug. The flat-screen TV on the wall was ginormous, and from the look of the stereo equipment it was all the latest stuff. It was set in a long, low entertainment unit, and there were surround-sound speakers hanging in strategic places on the walls.

She placed her hand on the wall separating the entryway from the living room as she wobbled, but sighed as she steadied and continued on. Sab loved the artwork on the wall, and when she saw a photo she changed direction and headed over to it.

Three men stood with their arms around each other's shoulders. Two of them were on either side of the guy in the middle, who looked a couple of years older, and the two on the outside of him had to be twins. They were all handsome and fit, and she felt her breasts tingle as they responded to their good-looking faces and brawny bodies, and she muttered under her breath at the unusual reaction.

When she heard laughing, she turned away from the photo and followed that sound. She noticed another hallway at the far side of the living room, which she guessed led to more bedrooms, but right now she needed to see who had taken her in. That was the only reason she could think of as to why she had woken up in someone's bedroom. Someone had kindly taken her in when she'd gotten sick. At least she hoped that was the way of it, because if it wasn't, she could be in deep shit.

Sab hesitated outside the kitchen door and listened to their deep, rumbling voices. She had a feeling she was about to encounter the three men she'd seen in the photo, and even though she was nervous, she took a deep breath, pushed her shoulders back, and stepped into the doorway. Nothing could have prepared her for seeing them in real life. They were all so tall, inches over six feet, and so damn handsome that her breath caught in her throat, choking her.

She covered her mouth when she started coughing, and the three men's gazes immediately zeroed in on her. The one on the stool slid off and rushed to her side. He pulled her into his arms and started patting her on the back.

"Are you okay, honey? What are you doing out of bed?" His deep voice rumbled against her ear, and shivers wracked her body. Her blood heated and so did her cheeks.

When she was finally able to stop coughing and pulled out of his arms, she was relieved that he let her go. The man's twin came up to stand beside his brother, and then he reached out and clasped her hand in his. His hand was so large it completely engulfed hers, and she couldn't believe how warm it felt against hers. But that wasn't all. When both of the men touched her, her body responded.

"Come and sit down, Sabrina. You really shouldn't be out of bed." He led her over to the table positioned on the other side of the room and pulled out a chair for her.

"Who are you?" she asked in a raspy voice. "Where am I?"

The three men sat down at the table. The twins took the seats either side of her, and the other man sat across from her. He was the one who started speaking. "My name is Trick Wendall, and these are my brothers Trent and Tristan. You're still in Slick Rock, but when you got sick and passed out, we decided to help you out and bring you home with us so you could recuperate."

"The doctor came and checked you over," Trent said. "You have the flu, honey."

"Thank you." She covered her mouth and coughed and then sniffed. "You wouldn't have any tissues handy, would you?"

Tristan got to his feet and hurried over to a sideboard she hadn't noticed, grabbed a box of tissues, and set them on the table in front of her. She grabbed a couple and blew her nose, and then when she spied the trash, she got up and disposed of them. She went to the sink and washed her hands.

"Do you want something to eat or drink?"

Sabrina spun around to find Trick leaning against the counter nearby. "Do you have any orange juice?"

He nodded, walked to the fridge, and got out the juice and then a glass from a cupboard, before pouring it into a glass and handing it to her.

"Thanks." Sabrina downed half the glass before coming up for air.

Trick clasped her wrist to hold the glass steady, topped it up, and then released her again then put the juice back in the fridge. He guided her back to the table, and she sighed when she sat down. She was feeling a little better but still had achy joints and a runny nose. She grabbed more tissues and wiped it.

"How are you feeling, Sabrina?" Tristan asked.

"Okay. I'm a little achy and my nose is runny, but other than that I'm fine."

"You had a really high fever. We had to put you in the bath to lower it," Trent said. "It seems to have done the trick." He placed his hand over her forehead and then winked at her before removing it again. "The fever's gone, sweetheart."

Her face heated when she realized that they had indeed seen her naked, but they had done it for medical reasons and not just to ogle her body.

"How do you know my name?"

"We found your wallet in your purse," Trick answered. "The doc needed to know if you had any medical conditions or if you were allergic to something." He leaned back in his chair and rubbed a hand over his face, and from his expression he looked a little guilty. "The sheriff ran a check on you."

It took a moment for those words to compute, but when they did, fear formed and lodged in her chest. She jumped to her feet and stumbled back. If Trent hadn't jumped up and snagged an arm around her waist she would have fallen over the chair behind her. She clutched at his arm and tried to get her terror under control, but she was breathing too fast, and because she was still unwell, dark spots formed in front of her eyes.

"Shh, honey, you're safe. Hold your breath for a moment and then exhale." Trent shifted her in his arms until she was standing side-on to his body and his hand rubbed up and down her back. "Good girl, now breathe out. There you go."

Sabrina leaned against him as her legs turned to mush. If he hadn't been holding her, she would have landed on the floor at his feet. She squeaked and gripped his shirt when he swept her up into his arms, and then he sat back down at the table, plonking her in his lap.

Her frantic mind began to slow, as did her heartbeat and breathing, and she was able to think a little more coherently.

"Why did you call the sheriff? You have no idea what you've done. He's going to come here and I'm going to die." Tears welled in her eyes and spilled over. Sabrina cursed her weakness, but she was so tired, everything was catching up with her, and being sick on top of it all, well, that didn't help.

She grabbed at the tissues and pulled some from the box, and buried her face in them. She tried so damn hard to stop crying, but the more she tried the harder it was. The tears seemed to flow from her eyes faster, and then she started sobbing. She was embarrassed over her emotional display, but the turmoil which had been roiling inside of her obviously needed to come out. She was aware of the silence and Trent's hand caressing up and down her back, over her head and hair, but she kept her cheek pressed against his chest and her eyes closed.

She didn't want to see the expressions on their faces. She'd heard how a woman's tears could make men uncomfortable, but that was the least of her worries right now. She didn't know what to do. She had no way of getting away from Slick Rock until the next bus out of town, and from what the bus driver had said that was at least a week from now. Oh, why didn't I ask where I was going? I've probably put these kind people in danger, too.

Finally her tears slowed, as did the sobs, until she was hiccupping. She reached for more tissues, keeping her gaze down, wiped her face, blew her nose, and then hopped up to discard the used tissues in the trash, and then she took the time to wash her hands at the sink again. By the time she was finished, she felt a little more in control and gazed at her reflection in the window over the sink. She couldn't really see herself properly but she didn't really need to. She sighed as she envisaged her red, bloodshot eyes, red nose, and shiny cheeks, but since there was nothing she could do about that, she mentally shrugged her shoulders and then made her way back to the table.

This time when she sat down, she took the seat at the end of the table. Now that she didn't have a man either side of her and one directly across from her she felt less hemmed in. She raised her head and jutted her chin out with attitude, just daring them to say anything about her breakdown, and waited.

She flinched when Trick's chair scraped on the floor as he pushed it back, and she watched as he got up, walked down the table, and took the seat to her left. He reached out, gripped her wrist, and placed her hand on the table palm up. The tip of his finger traced the lines of her hand, tickling her skin, but she didn't laugh. She was a little uncomfortable about having him touch her since they'd only just met, but she didn't say anything. He finally looked up and locked his brown eyes with hers.

"You're not going to die, Sabrina. My brothers and I will do everything we can to protect you." He released her from his gaze when he looked back down at her palm. "See this line here?" He traced the tip of his finger of the line, and she gasped when her hand began to tingle and goose bumps broke out all over her skin. "This is supposed to be your life line. From what I can see you haven't lived near long enough to be facing death."

Sabrina tried to pull her hand away, but his grip on her wrist tightened.

"You're going to have to tell us everything so we can keep you safe." Trick's words were a demand, but she wasn't sure it was a good idea to get him and his brothers involved in her problems.

She shook her head, and this time when she tugged at her hand he let her go. "The best thing I could do is to leave."

Trent got up from his seat and took the one to her right. Tristan also stood, but instead of moving to the empty chair next to Trent he walked up behind her and put his hands on her shoulders. Her already taut body tightened up even more. She wasn't used to being touched so much, and she began to wonder if these three men didn't care about invading her personal space or if they were just the type who liked to touch often.

When Tristan started massaging the tight muscles in her neck and shoulder, she couldn't help but groan at the pleasurable pain as they began to loosen and her head dropped forward. She inhaled deeply, and this time, when she moaned it was because of their clean, fresh scents and their close proximity. Her lids drifted closed, and she wished she hadn't closed her eyes, because their handsome, brawny images seemed to be burned into her mind's eye.

"You've been carrying around too much stress, baby," Tristan said as his thick, strong fingers dug into a particularly stubborn knot along her spine. "You need help and we're just the men to aid you."

Tears pricked her eyes again, but she didn't let them form. She took another deep breath and sighed as the tension in her muscles eased. She was so weary, and she was tempted to unload all her problems on these kind men, but she was also still a little wary.

Sabrina wanted to know why they were so eager to help her. What was in it for them? No one helped out nowadays, not unless there was some reward or monetary compensation. She didn't have the cash to be able to pay them to protect her.

Tristan's fingers stopped massaging her muscles since they had loosened up, but instead of moving away he stroked a hand over her head and down her messy hair. Then he lifted her and the chair she was sitting in away from the table, bent down, pushed an arm beneath her knees and the other around her shoulders, and lifted her up, and she gasped in surprise.

"What are you doing?" she asked in an almost breathless whisper and cursed at how dreamy her voice had sounded. Her throat was a little sore, and she hadn't meant to sound like she was trying to entice him, but that's what it had sounded like to her. She just hoped it didn't sound like that to him.

He smiled down at her and winked before he took her seat and lowered her onto his lap. "Just getting comfortable, baby. Trent, pass over her glass of juice. You have a sore throat don't you, Sab?"

"Yeah. Thanks," she said to Trent as he passed the glass to her. Sabrina picked it up and sipped a couple of times before placing it back on the table.

"Who is coming after you, Sabrina, and why?" Trick asked, and from the look on his face he wasn't about to let her put off answering any longer.

Sabrina decided the least she could do was to tell them why she was running. They had been so kind to her, and giving them information was the right thing to do. If the man or men after her found her, at least they would know what they were up against.

"I was Personal Assistant to Harvey Noble of Integrated Computers and Software." She paused to lick her lips and take another sip of her juice. "I accidentally opened an e-mail of his instead of forwarding it to his in-box like I had been requested to do. The information I read in that e-mail scared the hell out of me, and I was pretty sure Harvey hadn't seen me open his mail, but I couldn't be sure. He was walking past my desk when I'd read that mail, but when I looked up he didn't seem to be taking any notice of me. I marked that e-mail as unread and then forwarded it to him. I was lucky because it was time to knock off so I shut down my computer and left."

She took another deep breath and released it slowly, trying to circumvent the trembles that started in her belly. Tristan's arm wrapped around her waist and hugged her tight as if he were trying to offer her comfort and the strength to continue. She appreciated that because it had been so long since she'd felt another human being hugging her. The warmth from his body permeated hers, and she shifted slightly before continuing.

"I had to go back to the office a couple of hours later when I realized I'd left my cell phone in the desk drawer. I felt a little lost without it and didn't want to wait until the next morning before having it in my possession again.

"I didn't think anyone would be there since it was after office hours, but when I saw the light on in Harvey's office I quietly moved toward the door. He was on the phone to someone and when I realized what he was saying I knew he'd seen me open and read that e-mail."

Trent reached over and took her hand in his. She hadn't even noticed that her hands were fisted until he straightened her fingers out and laced their fingers together. She squeezed his hand like a lifeline when things felt so out of her control.

"What was he saying, Sabrina?" Trick asked.

Sabrina told them about the threats she overheard, and how she had destroyed her cell phone and run away with only the cash she could withdraw from the ATM.

"I went back to my car, drove to a secondhand car sales lot, sold it for cash, and hopped on the next bus out of Fort Collins."

"Did you plan your route?" Trent asked.

Sab shook her head. "I didn't care where I was going, just that it was away from my hometown. I purchased a couple of changes of clothes along the way and was lucky enough to be able to shower at the bus stations each day before getting on the next bus.

"I should have asked the drivers or the ticket sellers where the buses were going, but it didn't seem to matter. That was until I arrived here and found out there wasn't another bus for a week."

"Don't worry about that now, sweetheart." Trick leaned forward and rested his elbows on the table and looked at her intently. "What was in that e-mail, Sabrina?"

"It was an e-mail telling Harvey that one of the chips the company had made to spy on the FBI had fried and there was no way to get into the office to fix it unless something else went wrong with the computer." Sabrina gripped Trent's hand harder. "I think my boss has been placing spyware into all the computers he's sold. And believe me when I say that it is bad, that's an understatement. From what I could gather from the e-mail, he and his cronies can see every keystroke and e-mail coming and going from all the PCs he's put chips in. His company is huge, with stores all over the country, and he's sold a lot of computers. Even the White House has ordered a few."

"Fuck!" Trick roared, making her jump and whimper with fear. He stood up, his chair scraping on the floor, and when he reached for her she flinched and pulled back. He looked so angry, and for a moment she thought he might hit her.

Trick must have seen her reaction because the anger left his face and then he squatted down next to her and cupped her face in his hands. "Don't ever be scared of me or my brothers, sweetheart. I've never hit a woman before and I'm not about to start now. I'm not angry at you. I'm angry and worried about what Harvey Noble is up to." He leaned forward and kissed her softly on the lips.

Sabrina blinked, surprised yet oddly happy about him having kissed her. When she felt her areolae ruche and her nipples harden she crossed her arms over her chest. The action was uncomfortable and made her nipples ache even more when her limbs brushed over them. But what was more of a surprise was the way her pussy lips seemed to swell and moisten and her clit began throbbing.

Damn! These men are so frickin' potent they should come with a warning label.

Trick released her face and stood up. He moved over to the counter and removed his cell from his pocket before pressing a button, and he started talking.

"Luke, you and Damon need to get your asses over to our house." He paused as the other person must have started talking. "No. Right now!" Another pause. "Yes, it's bad. Do you know any feds or anyone in the White House?"

"No not over the phone. Just get over here, fast."

Yet another pause.

Chapter Four

"Don't you fucking tell me you can't find her," Harvey screamed into his phone. "I pay you good money to do as you're told. Hack into the bus terminal's security and see what you can find. I shouldn't have to tell you how to do your fucking job. Just fucking find her. Fast."

Harvey disconnected the call and very nearly hurled his cell phone across the room, but he didn't. He counted to fifty and breathed deeply until the rage burning inside him began to calm slightly. He was in deep shit, and if Sawyer didn't find that fucking bitch soon he was going to go down. But Harvey was going to make damn sure he took Sawyer with him. He knew he was being watched by the law. Probably the fucking feds as well as the CIA, and he could practically feel the walls closing in around him and hear the bar doors of a jail cell slamming closed behind him.

He'd gone into hiding and hadn't used his usual cell or his credit cards. He was so glad he'd set up a fake persona a couple of months after the first sale of one of his computers with those chips in them. He knew he should have been happy with the billion-plus dollars he was reportedly worth, but a lot of that money was tied up in his company and he only had a few million in cash accounts. A man could never have too much money or power, and when the idea of that chip had formed, he had spent months perfecting it. He wasn't about to let the law get in his way. He lived in America, the land of the free, and should be able to do anything he damn well pleased.

He smirked as he thought about the information he had downloaded from the computer chips to his own PC and the terabyte hard drives he'd hidden away with that information on them. Even the White House wasn't safe, and the damning information he had on some of the politicians and a few high-powered, prominent businessmen could make him a lot more money. In a way, he was glad that the president was on the up and up, but he wondered what the commander in chief would do if he found out some of his senators were dirty. Probably kick them to the curb and throw the book at them.

He rubbed his hands together as he remembered the anonymous e-mails he'd sent out to those dirty fuckers. He would have loved to have been a fly on the wall when they had known they'd been caught. He could see it now. The sweat beading on their faces and them scrambling to try and cover their tracks, but it was too late. Harvey had ordered them to pay money into a numbered Swiss account to keep his mouth shut. Those fuckers had wrought the system while being in positions of government. Each of them using their privileges in ways they shouldn't have. One asshole was getting cut backs from the building industry and using inside knowledge to buy up land. He was pretty sure there would be a riot if the public found out one of the politicians was using taxpayers' money to pay for high-class call girls regularly.

Another was using his position to get free flights to anywhere in the world for him and his family. He wondered if the asshole's wife knew what he was doing. Doubtful.

There were so many people in this country trying to survive in poverty. Not that Harvey gave a shit, but he knew the citizens of America would. If any of the information he had came out, there would be an uproar.

Potus might even be usurped since he was supposed to know what was going on in his own party and had no clue. Of course it wasn't the president's fault that the treasurer was skimming funds from the country's coffers, or any of the other stuff for that matter, but the public would crucify him if anyone knew.

Harvey stared at the stained walls of the seedy motel and muttered a curse. Once Sawyer found and got rid of Sabrina, Harvey was skipping out. He had over a hundred grand in cash in the duffel bag in the closet with his false papers. He'd even taken the measures of changing his appearance. He'd shaved his head and bought clear glasses, and he'd brought chain store clothes. He hated the way the cheap fabric felt on his skin when he was used to quality, but he would put up with it until he could escape, even if it took a few months.

He was planning on buying a one-way ticket to Switzerland and from there...the world would be his oyster. Harvey was worried that the feds and CIA knew what he'd done, but he wasn't sure. Hopefully they had been watching Sawyer because of Sawyer's reputation and his long rap sheet. There was no way the authorities could know about the chip unless that bitch had told someone. No. He didn't think she'd have the guts to rat him out. She was a weak woman and had run. He needed Sawyer to find her, but from the way things were going, he wasn't holding his breath.

Harvey had met Sawyer in a bar one night, and after finding out what he did for a living, he'd hired him on the spot. Sawyer had been a bodyguard, and he'd found out after that the asshole also had a rap sheet a mile long. He'd been questioned for murder but hadn't been arrested for it. His hireling had been charged and spent time in the slammer for assault, robbery, and dealing drugs, but Harvey didn't give a damn. He'd figured that having a man like Sawyer on his team would come in handy, and he'd been right.

Sawyer wasn't only a muscular thug, he was a geek, too. His expertise had come in handy with all the spyware Harvey had out in America. Sawyer had been helping him keep watch and download stuff on those assholes in the White House and the FBI, as well as the one lone computer they had in the CIA.

But the heat was on now, and he could almost feel the authorities breathing down his neck, and it was all his bitch of an ex-assistant's fault. It had to be. He didn't think anyone else in his company knew what was going on, but unless he interrogated all of his employees, he couldn't be certain, and that would take way too long.

He wasn't a stupid man, and he decided going into hiding would be more prudent than hanging around and waiting for the shit to hit that fan. He'd told one of the other office managers that he had a family emergency and had taken off. He just hoped that he didn't have to spend too long hiding in seedy motels, because he was used to living with the best.

It had to be that fucking bitch's fault. She was a damn mouse, but he hadn't expected the slut to run. She had to have told someone in the law what she'd read in that fucking e-mail. Although he had no proof of that and Sawyer was probably on the authority's alert list, he felt like the net was closing in around him.

Harvey wasn't about to give up without taking Sabrina out. If Sawyer could manage to do that without Harvey having to get his hands dirty, he may very well be able to get away without being sent to jail. Sawyer was going to be his scapegoat even if he didn't know it. There was no way he was going down if he could help it. With Sawyer's background, it would be easy to point the finger at him and pretend innocence, but only if the fucker didn't work out that he was using him, too. If that happened then Harvey could see Sawyer coming after him, and he knew, if he did, there would be no prison bars. He would end up six feet under.

He'd been trying to track his naïve ex-assistant and hadn't had any more luck than Sawyer had, but Harvey wasn't about to give up.

He sat staring at the program he'd been running for the last two weeks from his seedy motel room and was just about to give up for the day when an alert went off. His fingers flew across the keyboard, and he smiled coldly when he found that the Slick Rock sheriff's department had just done a check on Sabrina. Relaxing back in his chair, he rubbed his hands together and then he started laughing.

Got you, you bitch.

Harvey picked up his burner phone and sent Sawyer the details.

Sabrina was going to die very soon, even if he had to kill the bitch himself.

* * * *

Tristan could hardly comprehend what Sabrina had just told them about Harvey Noble. He was glad that she had run and ended up in Slick Rock, but he was scared for her. Harvey Noble and his cohorts weren't going to give up looking for her until they had found and killed her.

At the moment, she was sitting at the kitchen table with a red nose and shiny cheeks and he could see she was flagging, her energy spent because of her illness, and no doubt from being on the run. He wanted to be able to tell her to go back to bed, but they were waiting on Luke and Damon to arrive so they could figure out what to do.

Even though she was trying to be brave and her expression was stoic, at the moment when his gaze met hers, he could see the deep-seated fear in those gorgeous blue orbs. He wanted to wrap her up in his arms and never let go, but she'd only just met them, and with everything else going on, he wasn't sure she'd accept any overtures from him, either sexual or just of a comforting nature. She had spent the last ten or so minutes staring at the now-empty glass of juice, and he could see by the occasional frown that her mind was racing, and her body language had "keep off" signs all over it. Her shoulders were hunched, rounded, and whenever he, Trent, or Trick moved near her she shifted away.

He wanted to know what she was thinking, but somehow he already had a clue where her mind was wandering. There was no way he was letting her leave and spend the rest of her life alone and on the run, constantly looking over her shoulder and never having the chance to settle down. Nor did he think going into witness protection was an option. He had no doubt that Luke and Damon would suggest it, but since Noble was as rich as Croesus, that wasn't exactly safe either. That asshole could have bought off cops, feds, and anyone else he deemed necessary to keep on his payroll to continue his scam.

What Tristan wanted to know was why that fucker had done what he had. Did he have plans of selling national secrets? Or maybe he just wanted dirt on other prominent officials to blackmail them. No, that didn't make sense either. The man had more money than anyone could spend in a lifetime from what he'd heard, but if it was all tied up in the business maybe he wanted more. He shook his head mentally. There had to be another reason that bastard was spying on their country. Didn't there? Surely greed and power weren't the only motivating factors in Noble's actions. But Tristan knew men had killed for a lot less and the possibility of cash could be a powerful motivator for some people.

The knock on the front door had Trick hurrying toward it, and then he was back with Luke and Damon.

Tristan sat beside Sabrina and nudged her arm gently. "Do you want some more juice, baby?"

"No, thanks, but a cup of coffee would be nice."

Tristan got up and hurried over to the freshly brewed pot and came back to the large table with mugs, cream, and sugar. Luke sat in the seat across from Sab, and Damon sat beside him. Both of them glanced at her, but she didn't acknowledge them. Once more she was staring, but this time at the tabletop since he'd removed the empty glass.

He took a seat beside her, and Trick sat to her other side. Trent sat next to Tristan, and he could see that his brother was worried about Sabrina, just like he was. Trick covered the hand she had resting on the tabletop, and after lacing their fingers together, he brought her hand down to rest on his thigh while still holding it.

Tristan poured the coffee and handed the mugs out before pushing the cream and sugar toward Sabrina, but she shook her head before tugging her hand free of Trick's and wrapped both her hands around the mug as if they were cold. She finally looked like she was back with them instead of lost in her head, and she nodded to Luke and Damon.

"Sabrina, these two men are the town sheriffs," Trick began. "This is Luke Sun-Walker and Damon Osborn. Guys, Sabrina Brown."

"Sheriffs."

"Call us Luke and Damon, ma'am." Damon smiled, clearly trying to put her at ease.

She tried to smile back, but failed when the smile didn't reach her eyes. "Please call me Sabrina, Sabby, or Sab. All my friends do."

"Can you tell us what the problem is, Sabrina?" Luke asked.

Sabrina began to explain, and the more she spoke, the more worried the town sheriffs looked.

"Jesus," Damon said and scrubbed a hand over his face.

Luke looked pale instead of his normal bronze tone, and his mouth pulled tight as he leaned his elbows on the table.

"My office is lucky enough not to have Noble's computers, but I may have put you in more danger." Luke paused to take a sip of coffee and swallowed audibly as if his throat were tight.

"Yes," Sabrina sighed. "I figured that out when the guys told me you ran a check on me when I got sick and passed out at the diner." Her knuckles turned white as she gripped the mug tighter. "I think the best thing for everyone in this town would be for me to move on."

"No!" Tristan, Trick, and Trent said simultaneously.

Sabrina turned to meet each of their gazes before looking back at Luke and Damon. "If Harvey Noble is looking for me and has alerts set up on his computer then he is going to send someone or come after me himself. I would be putting everyone in this town in danger."

Luke cleared his throat. "I don't think you're going to be safe anywhere, Sabrina. He is going to hunt you down until he finds you. He's not going to give up. Surely you don't want to spend the rest of your life on the run?"

"What choice do I have?" Sabrina asked, her voice becoming strident and then cracking on the last word. "Do you think I could live with my conscience if some innocent person in this town got hurt or ended up dead because he's after me? I can't do that. I just can't."

Sabrina pushed away from the table and hurried from the room. Tristan saw the tears streaming down her face before she left the kitchen. He immediately rose to his feet and went after her. He was concerned she would try to make a run for it, but that wasn't an option. He didn't give a shit if he had to spend every cent they had and hire a contingency of bodyguards to keep her safe. He knew deep down inside, in his heart, that Sabrina was meant to be theirs, and he couldn't let her leave. No way. No how. Her leaving wasn't going to happen.

He searched the house and sighed with relief when he found her in the master bedroom, lying on the bed crying her eyes out. She tried to muffle the sobs with her head under the pillow, but he could see her whole body shaking as she cried. His heart ached at the fear and turmoil she must be feeling. He felt just as tumultuous, but he wasn't about to let his emotions rule. He needed to keep it together for Sabrina. He needed to help her to calm down and to stop and think before making any rash decisions, but his first priority was calming her.

He kicked his shoes off and then climbed up behind her before wrapping her in his arms and pulling her against his body. She stiffened and then relaxed in his hold. He didn't say anything but just continued to hold her until finally the tears slowed and the hiccupping lessened. Slowly but surely, her breathing evened out and her body grew lax, and he knew she was asleep. He lifted the pillow from over her head and gently brushed the blonde strands of hair back off her face. She didn't stir, and he knew she'd exhausted herself, plus she still wasn't well.

Tristan didn't want to leave her alone. He wanted to continue holding her so she wouldn't wake up alone, but he needed to hear what they were going to do. He went to the closet, grabbed a quilt from the cupboard, and covered her with it, before placing a light kiss on her cheek and heading out.

He sat down and faced Trick. "Does the bank have any of Noble's computers?"

"No," Trick answered.

"Is there any way we can get an expert to get hold of one of their computers and search for that chip?" Tristan questioned.

Trent nodded toward Luke, who was currently speaking quietly on his cell in the kitchen. "Luke has a couple of buddies in the FBI and is giving them a heads-up. Hopefully someone there will be able to find what they're looking for and get things rolling to arrest the asshole."

Tristan sighed and nodded. "It won't make a difference if they are able to indict Noble. Whoever he contacted about Sab is probably already on their way here. We have no idea who or how many assholes he's sent to come after her. I'd bet my last dollar it will be more than one."

Luke ended his call and came back to the table. "Justin Dumont is checking into it. He works at FBI Headquarters in Washington, DC. They have a few computers in the human-relations section which came from Noble."

"Shit!" Damon slumped in his chair. "That means that Noble probably knows all the agents' names, where they live, and anything else he'd want to know. What the hell is he up to?"

"That's the million-dollar question, isn't it?" Luke sighed. "The only thing I can come up with is power and money. It doesn't matter to some people how rich they are."

"How is Sabrina?" Trick asked, changing the subject.

"She was crying her heart out, but she's asleep for now," Tristan answered.

"What the hell do we do?" Trent asked. "How the hell do we keep her safe?"

"She needs to change her appearance first and foremost," Damon said. "We can get our women on board to help out. I'll get Rachel to buy some hair dye and maybe you can get Felicity to get some colored contacts for her."

"Good idea," Luke said.

Tristan was pleased that the two lawmen were going to ask their wives to help make Sabrina look different. He hated having to do that because she was beautiful just the way she was, but hopefully, by changing her appearance, when the assholes sent to kill her came, they wouldn't recognize her. He wanted her to have every chance she could to survive and hide.

"I think you all should come and stay out at the ranch," Luke said. "We can protect her better away from town, and if these fuckers find her at least no one in town will be in the line of fire."

"Wait," Trick said. "You could be putting Flick and the kids in danger. I don't think that's a good idea."

Luke rubbed his chin and frowned before he nodded in agreement. "You're right. I don't want my family in danger."

"What about the Heritage Ranch, to the southwest?" Damon asked. "The three Heritage brothers were SEALs, but took over the ranch after their folks retired to warmer climes."

"Yes," Trick said. "I know David, Barry, and Hank Heritage, well. They come into the bank often. Plus, they don't have any woman or kids to worry about. Let me call Hank now and see if he's okay with us staying with them."

Trick made the call, and after explaining what was going on, he smiled and gave the thumbs-up. "Okay, thanks, Hank. We'll be out to your place in a few hours. Do you want me to bring anything?" Trick paused and waited for a reply. "Sure, no worries. We'll bring enough food to last the seven of us quite a while." He disconnected the call. "That's a go.

"I'll organize my second in charge to take over at the bank." He met Tristan's and Trent's eyes. "You don't have any jobs for a few weeks, do you?"

"No." Trent shook his head. "We intended to have some downtime. It's getting colder and we've finished the jobs we had going. Since we've been working non-stop for the last two years, it was more than time to take a breather."

"Thank fuck for that," Trick muttered. "The more of us protecting Sabrina, the better.

"Trent, I want you and Tristan to get a heap of supplies, and don't forget to pick up some clothes and other things she'll need. I want to be out at the Triple H Ranch before sundown and don't want to have to come back here unless absolutely necessary. I'll pack you both a bag and meet you at Hank's place."

Luke and Damon stood. "I'll let you know if Justin finds anything and if he's able to bring Noble in for questioning."

"I'd appreciate it," Trick said as he rose to his feet. "Do you think Dumont will inform all the other agencies?"

"You can count on it," Luke replied. "I'll bet as soon as I hung up he was calling the CIA and anyone else he could think of."

Tristan stood up and went to the drawer they kept a pad and pens in then removed both items. He looked at Trent. "Help me figure out what we're going to need in town. It's better we write a list before heading out. I don't want to forget anything."

When they'd finished, the lettersize page was full with everything he and Trent could think they'd need, from food and drinks to clothes for Sabrina. Tristan hated shopping, but he would do anything to make their woman's life easier, and he knew it was going to take a few hours to get everything together.

"What's going on?"

Tristan looked toward the doorway to see Sabrina leaning against the frame and looking sleep flushed. Her face was a healthy pink color, and although her hair was hanging around her head in disarray, to him she was sexy and beautiful.

Trent moved before he could and didn't stop until he pulled her into his arms. Tristan watched as her eyes slid closed, and then she looped her arms around his brother's waist and snuggled in. He smiled, happy that she seemed to be becoming more comfortable with their displays of affection and settling in a little more. His brother looked happier than a pig in shit.

Since they were standing side on, he could see both Trent's and Sabrina's faces, and they both looked content. Although content was too weak a word where Trent was concerned. His smile was nearly wide enough to crack his face. He leaned down and kissed the top of her head and then he inhaled deeply, and he smelled her fresh, clean, womanly scent.

His dick twitched in his pants. He didn't have to be close to her to remember what she smelled like or what she felt like when he'd been holding her. She was it for him and his brothers. The one and only woman they wanted to spend the rest of their lives loving and holding.

Tristan smiled at her when her lids popped open. Trent led her over to the counter and seated her on a stool.

"We are going to be staying at a friend's ranch for a while," Tristan said. "We were just compiling a list of everything we're going to need to see us through."

"Oh. Okay." Sabrina turned to look out the window, her shoulders slumping when her head turned. She reached up to her hair, but instead of pushing it back like he thought she would, she brought it further forward as if she were trying to hide from them.

Trent sat on the stool next to her and raised an eyebrow at him in question, but since Tristan had no idea what was wrong, he shrugged.

Trick entered the kitchen after seeing Luke and Damon out and smiled when he saw her sitting on the stool, but the smile faded when Tristan shook his head. He and Trent both raised their hands slightly trying to tell Trick that something was wrong with Sabrina but they didn't know what. Thank God they knew each other so well, because from the frown that crossed his brother's face, Trick understood.

"Sabrina, are you all right, sweetheart?" Trick moved around until he was standing behind her.

"Yeah, I'm fine. If it's okay with you, I'd like to have a shower before I leave."

Trick clasped her shoulders and turned her on the swivel seat until she was facing him. "Leave? Why are you leaving? I thought we'd already decided that it was safer for you to stay with us."

"But—"

"Ah shit." Tristan realized she'd gotten the wrong impression when he said they were getting ready to leave for a friend's ranch. He hurried around the counter until he was standing next to Trick and cupped her face between his hands. "Baby, you're coming with us."

"I am?" Her question was asked in a quiet voice, and then her lower lip trembled and he noticed the glint of moisture in her eyes. That nearly undid him. To see her so emotional and unsure was like having a knife stabbed into his heart.

He nudged Trick aside and lifted her up against his chest. She hooked her arms around his neck and her legs around his waist. She looked so scared and vulnerable, but also beautiful and sexy. His body hardened, his cock filled with blood, and his balls swelled. He couldn't hold back with her anymore. He needed to know what she tasted like, needed to feel connected to her physically as well as emotionally.

Tristan held her gaze as he lowered his head slowly. Her eyes widened slightly before her lids drooped in an unconscious sexy come-on that he couldn't ignore. His lips met hers, lightly, softly, as he brushed them back and forth, testing her acceptance of him. Her lips parted as she exhaled, and then he changed the angle of his head and devoured her.

His tongue entered her mouth and slid along and around hers. He loved the sexy little whimpering sounds she made as he kissed her and kissed her some more. Her arms tightened around his neck, and her legs gripped his waist. Without taking his mouth from hers or opening his eyes, he nudged the stool away and lowered her ass to the granite counter before gripping her hips and pulling her covered pussy against his jeans-covered erection. She moaned and he growled as she rocked her hips against his hard cock.

It would have been so much better if they had been naked and he had been buried deep inside her wet heat, but he was already pushing his luck by kissing her so hungrily. Tristan had never been so starving for anyone before and knew no matter how much he kissed her or touched her, it would never be enough. He would never get tired of kissing or loving her, but she still had no idea that he and his brothers wanted to have a relationship with her. He couldn't, wouldn't do anything more than he already was before they told her what they wanted.

With a regretful moan, Tristan withdrew his tongue from her mouth and eased the intensity of the kiss down until he was sipping at her lips. Finally he made himself lift his head, but instead of moving back he pressed his forehead to hers. They were both breathing rapidly, and it was damn hard not to give in to his desires and take her mouth beneath his all over again. His breathing finally slowed, and as he loosened his hold on her hips, her legs dropped from around his waist and her arms unhooked from around his neck. He took a step back, but she wouldn't meet his gaze, so he took her chin in his thumb and finger to gently force her head up.

Pink crept up her cheeks and she tried to glance away, but he wasn't about to let her. "Why are you embarrassed about what we shared, Sabrina?"

She glanced off to the side and then her lids lowered, but the pink hue in her cheeks became more pronounced.

"Look at me, baby," he ordered and was pleased when she complied. "My brothers and I are very attracted to you. We want to have a relationship with you."

Her eyes widened with shock, and then she looked over to Trick and Trent with narrowed eyes. He saw incredulity in her gaze, but that wasn't all. There was also anger. Her mouth opened as if to refute his claim, but he placed his finger over her lips before she spoke.

Trick moved in closer, and Tristan released her chin before stepping back slightly. He didn't have to look to his left at Trent. His brother hadn't moved away since he'd started kissing her. He had no doubt that he was just waiting for his moment, for his first taste of Sabrina, too.

Trick reached for her hand and threaded their fingers together. "Slick Rock is known for its acceptance of out-of-the-norm relationships. The people in this town don't judge or slander anything or anyone that's different."

Trent placed his hand on her knee and squeezed. "There are a lot of polyamorous relationships here, darlin'. Luke, the sheriff, shares his wife with his good friends Tom and Billy Eagle. Damon and his brothers Sam and Tyson are married to Rachel."

Tristan decided it was time he had a little input, too. "As far as we know there are eleven polyandrous families in this town. It feels like we've been waiting a lifetime for the right woman to come into our lives, baby."

"And we believe you are that woman," Trick said in a calm, confident voice.

Chapter Five

Sabrina could barely comprehend what they were saying. Her brain was fried after such a passionately carnal kiss. She was so damned horny her insides were quaking and her panties were soaked through.

The words each of the men had spoken echoed through her mind, and the more she heard them, the more she wanted to reach out and grab hold of them. At first she'd thought they were joking, but not in a humorous way. She'd thought they were playing some sort of game with her, but as she looked from one man to the other she could see they were totally serious and sincere.

She'd never felt pulled in so many different directions at once and had no idea what to do, or what to think, or what to say. And how could she even consider having a relationship with one man, let alone three, when her life was in danger? She didn't know how many tomorrows she had left, and if she started something with them and one of them got hurt, she couldn't bear it.

Sabrina felt like she was walking around with a target painted in the middle of her forehead and wondered, if she listened hard enough, if she could hear the clock ticking down.

The silence in the room wasn't comfortable. It was pregnant with tense expectation, and when she looked at the three men again she saw them watching her with apprehensive anticipation. Her throat constricted, and she gulped loudly before taking a deep breath and exhaling.

"I don't…I can't…" Sabrina snapped her mouth shut when the words wouldn't come. She had no idea what to say to their declaration.

Trick stepped forward, scooped her up into his arms, and hugged her tight. "Don't say anything yet, darlin'. You need to think about what you want before answering."

Sabrina sighed as she wrapped her arms around his neck. He lowered her feet to the floor, and even though she knew she should release him, she didn't want to. She'd never felt safer than when she was in his, Trent's, or Tristan's arms, but she knew she couldn't stay where she was forever.

She made a conscious effort to drop her arms and move away from him, and when she did, she bumped into another hard, warm body. She looked up and met Trent's eyes, and without saying a word to her, he gave her a slight smile and opened his arms. She didn't hesitate to walk into them, and she gripped the front of his shirt and sighed when his arms enveloped her. She breathed in his delectable scent and sighed with enjoyment and contentment. She wished she could accept having a relationship with them, but with her future so uncertain it wouldn't be fair to any of them.

Trent kissed the top of her head just before he released her, and then he and Tristan headed out to go shopping.

She spent the next couple of hours helping Trick pack up some clothes for them and clearing out the fridge of any perishables. They worked together in silence before her curiosity got the better of her.

"What do you and your brothers do for a living?"

He glanced over at her and smiled before he went back to pull more clothes from the drawers in Trent's room. "We own the only bank in town. Our parents started that bank before any of us were born, and when they died in an accident I took it over.

"Tristan and Trent didn't want to work in the bank though. They like working with their hands and started up their own construction business after finishing college."

"I'm sorry about your parents," Sabrina said when she saw the sadness in his eyes. He gave her a wistful smile and stroked a finger down her face. "Thanks, honey, but it was a long time ago."

"How old were you when you took over running the bank?"

"I was twenty." He shook his head and then grinned. "Boy, did I grow up fast. I thought I could walk right in and just take on over, but that was so far from the truth it's almost funny. Thank God my dad's best friend, Charlie, was there to help me. He took me under his wing and taught me the ropes. If it hadn't been for him, I may have lost the lot."

"Do you still see your dad's friend?"

"No, but I get mail from him occasionally. He moved to California to be closer to this daughter and grandkids. Last I heard, he was having the time of his life."

Sabrina nodded before adding the stack of clothes she'd chosen for Trent into the large bag on the bed.

"How did you come to work for Noble?" Trick asked.

She hoped he didn't see the way she tightened up but figured he had when he frowned. It wasn't that she had anything to hide, it was just that she didn't really like to think of Harvey Noble and his cronies. Every time she did her stomach began to churn and she felt sick with fear, but she wasn't about to let Noble rule her life when he wasn't even here. So she pushed her fear aside.

"I'd just finished up college after getting my business management degree. I'd been searching the Internet and papers for work, and when I saw the advertisement for an administrative assistant to the CEO of Noble Computers I immediately applied for the job." Sabrina added another pile of folded clothes to Trent's bag and then walked to the closet in search of a spare pair of shoes. She found and then picked up the boots for Trick's approval and, at his nod, put them in the separate zippered section under the lid.

"When I had the initial interview I didn't think I'd have a hope in hell of getting the position. I was kind of nervous and thought I hadn't done as well as I could have. Harvey was good at hiding what he was thinking and feeling, but I had this feeling he thought I was naïve, and looking back now, I can see that I was. Maybe that's what he wanted. Someone young and stupid he could push around." Tears burned the back of her eyes, but she pushed her emotions aside.

She sometimes felt so out of her depth with Trick and his brothers. They were so much more mature than she was, and since her self-esteem was a little low with what was happening with Noble, she was uncertain of trusting her instincts. She wanted to accept Trick, Trent, and Tristan's offer of a relationship, but knew this wasn't the time, and she was unsure of why they wanted her. She was a fair bit younger than they were, and she was feeling the age difference right now.

Although, it was very tempting to say yes. They were all so handsome, manly, and masculine, but she hadn't had much experience with relationships and didn't want to come across as too eager or make a fool of herself.

Sabrina had been a confident career woman, but now she had no career and had begun to think that Noble had only hired her for his own nefarious reasons. When he'd told her not to open any of his e-mails but instead to send them on to him, her alarm bells should have been ringing. She'd thought it was odd at the time but had put it down to Harvey being a bit of a control freak and hadn't questioned it. Now she wished she'd trusted her first instinct and questioned him, but he probably would have made up so cockamamie story she would have naively believed.

Trick came up behind her and pulled her back against his front. She was so damn tired she wanted to lean on him and his brothers, but she couldn't do that. Not now and maybe not ever. What she really should be doing was walking away.

"You're not stupid, sweetheart. How were you supposed to know what he was up to?"

"I should have realized something was up." She took a deep breath and stepped to the side and watched as Trick closed the bag, and then she followed him out of Trent's room. She headed into Tristan's room and began opening drawers and pulling out clothes.

"What do you mean, Sab?"

"Harvey told me that if any e-mails to him came through the company e-mail address that I wasn't supposed to open them and just forward them on to him. At first I thought that was unusual, but in the end I put it down to him being a control freak or just being overly conscientious."

"Did you think something strange was going on?"

"Sometimes. A couple of times he got visitors that were intimidating and rough looking, but I tried not to let it bother me. People come from all walks of life and have harsher upbringings than others, and I just put it down to that. He always had security around him or a bodyguard, but with him making so much money that wasn't a surprise.

"I caught him looking at me weirdly a couple of times, but when he caught me watching him, he'd change his expression and smile at me. But his smile never reached his eyes and he always looked kind of cold. Sometimes I swear there was…not evil in his eyes, but a kind of manic determination. That's the only way I can describe it."

"Can you describe his bodyguard? Did you see any of his men?"

Sabrina shook her head. "I can tell you now that his bodyguards were contractors hired from a reputable company. I was the one who handled hiring them for him. His men, I don't think I ever saw. He used to set up a lot of his business meetings outside of office hours. I thought that was odd but didn't question it since he always seemed so busy.

"I asked him once early on about the late meetings and the look that came into his eyes scared me, but he just shrugged it off, saying he had a couple of small businesses he was planning to open but didn't want the media to get ahold of that information. I just took him for his word. It could have been true and I just shrugged of the misgivings I had."

"So you only found out what he was up to after you accidentally opened one of his e-mails?" Trick asked, and she nodded. "You know if the people he was working with and who were working for him didn't want the law to find out what was going on, you'd think they would have had his personal e-mail address."

Sabrina closed the bag once it was full of Tristan's clothes with an extra pair of boots inside plus all of his toiletries. She went to lift it off of the bed but Trick nudged her aside and picked it up himself. She followed him out as he carried the bag to the internal garage door before he turned around to face her again.

"You know I think that whoever sent that e-mail wanted Noble to be caught. Do you know who it came from?"

"No. It was one of those made-up names."

"Can you remember what the name was, sweetheart?"

"Yes. It was kind of creepy and hard to forget."

"Tell me what it was and I'll text it to Luke. Maybe his friend in the FBI can track the person down."

"Eye of the devil dot com."

Trick pulled his cell from his pocket and started tapping at the screen and replaced it when he'd finished. "Go and get your bag, sweetheart. I'll load the bags and cooler into the truck and then we can head out."

"What about Tristan and Trent?"

"They're heading straight to the Triple H Ranch when they're done shopping."

"Okay." She sighed as she turned around and headed for the bedroom where her small bag was. She hated that the three Wendall brothers were putting their lives on hold because of her, and even though she felt safer with them, she wondered if she was being selfish.

Maybe being at their friend's ranch would give her a place to think and decide what to do. It didn't matter that she no longer had a car. If she decided to leave she would walk out. Noble and his cronies wouldn't be looking for anyone on foot. She was sure they would scour the bus depots, airlines, car-rental places, and anything else they could think of.

She was just glad that she'd taken the precaution of not leaving a paper trail and hoped that it was enough to keep her hidden. But deep down she knew that she wasn't safe no matter where she went. Harvey Noble wasn't going to give up until her found her and killed her.

Sabrina grabbed her backpack and walked back through the house. She could hear Trick moving around in the garage, probably still loading everything in it. This would be the perfect opportunity to take off. She could run and hide so that he and his brothers and their friends were safe.

She took a step toward the front door, but spun around when Trick spoke. "Ready?"

He was frowning at her, and she wondered if he knew what she'd been about to do, but when he smiled at her and held out his hand, she didn't think so. Sabrina walked closer to him, took his hand, and hoped she wasn't making a big mistake.

He took her bag from her and stowed it into the backseat before making sure the house was locked up, and then he helped her into the front passenger seat before starting the truck and backing out of the four-car garage. She watched the automatic doors close, and then she was scanning the streets and other cars she saw as he drove.

There was no way she could let her guard down. Not until she was safe. She was going to have to stay vigilant, even if it meant staying awake at night. Her chest tightened, and her heart began to race. Her throat tightened as she panted and sweat broke out on her forehead. She gripped her hands and tried to calm down, but she couldn't seem to control the escalating panic.

She was glad that Trick had the radio on and didn't seem to know what was happening to her. She kept her head turned away as she stared out the side window and tried to take in the scenery as they left the small rural town behind. After lowering the window a crack and breathing in the fresh cool afternoon fall air, she felt her body begin to relax, and her heart slowed, as did her breathing.

"Are you all right, honey?" Trick asked.

When she turned to face him she saw him frowning with concern. "Yes, thanks. I'm fine."

He faced the road again but glanced at her a few times before speaking again. "You're as pale as a ghost, Sabrina. Talk to me, sweetheart. Are you worried about all of us wanting a relationship with you?"

"Yes. No. I don't know. I'm just kind of confused right now."

Trick slowed the truck, pulled onto the shoulder of the road, and then turned the ignition off. He released his seatbelt before doing the same with hers and turned so he was facing her. She shifted in her seat until she was facing him, too.

"Tell me what's going on in that mind of yours."

"I don't want anyone getting hurt because of me. You, your brothers, and now your friends at the ranch we're heading to, are putting your lives on hold. None of us know if Noble's hired goon will find me, and it could take weeks or even months before they do. I should just pack up and leave."

Trick shifted along the bench seat and reached out for her. He pulled her over toward him and wrapped her up in his embrace. "Firstly, we want to keep you safe. My brothers and I are very attracted to you, and we want the chance to see where the attraction between all of us can go."

She opened her mouth but didn't get to say anything when he placed a finger over her lips. She had the wildest urge to draw that finger into her mouth and suck on it. Her cheeks heated, and her body lit up with desire.

"See." Trick's deep rumbling voice vibrated against her side and shot straight down to her clit. "That's what I'm talking about, honey. Those sparks we light off in one another are a rare thing. Don't you want to explore the passion between us?"

Sabrina had every intention of shaking her head, but it seemed her body and mind were disconnected and she found herself nodding instead. She felt her eyes widen in shock and tried to pull back, but Trick wouldn't let her.

"I won't let you take that back, Sabrina. Now the issue you have about us putting our lives on hold. Do you really think we would do something we didn't want to?

"Trent and Tristan had already planned to take a couple of weeks off. They'd finished all the jobs they had scheduled and were looking forward to some down time. Me"—he paused as if trying to find the right words and stroked a finger down her cheek—"I'm a workaholic, sweetheart. If I'm not at the bank, I'm at the baby and mom's store helping Tori out. We went into partnership when one of her friends said that she hated driving two hours away from home just to get things she needed for her babies. That was over eighteen months ago, and other than taking Sundays as a rest day, I've been working every day of the week for years. Tori and I don't have any need to go to the store. We have reliable employees who can run that shop like a well-oiled machine. As for the bank, my second in charge has been urging me to take some vacation time for so long that he's probably in shock since I have done just that. He can run that place just as well as I can.

"As for you leaving, that's not an option. We can keep you safe here. This town is full of men who look out for their women. If I saw one of the other men's wives in trouble you can bet your ass I'd be there to help out. That goes for everyone in this town. We protect our own."

"But I'm not—"

"Don't you dare finish that statement, Sabrina! The moment you collapsed in the diner you became one of ours. You have been in our house recovering for the last couple of days, and as far as I'm concerned you already belong to me and my brothers."

He didn't even give her time to reply to that because he leaned down and covered her mouth with his. She moaned as she clutched at his shirt, and his tongue pushed into her mouth, gliding along and swirling around hers. She was lost to his touch, his taste, his passion. He didn't cajole a response from her. He dove right in and took what he wanted. His lips were soft and warm, yet firm and demanding. His tongue pushed in and out of her mouth, turning her limbs to rubber and starting a fire burning low in her belly. She wanted to taste him for the rest of her life. To have his arms around her keeping her safe.

When that thought crossed her mind, Sabrina knew she was in deeper than she'd first thought. How could three men get under her skin so quickly? It scared her a little, but not enough to make her run. No, she wanted to hold on and never let go.

She groaned with frustrated disappointment when Trick slowed the kiss and lifted his head. The hunger in his eyes burned into her soul as well as her body. She shivered and clenched her thighs together, trying to ease the ache in her pussy.

"The Heritage men are trained SEALs, honey. Damon and his brothers were Marines. There are a lot of men in this town that served in the military. If Noble's men try to get near you, they are going to have a very hard time."

Trick helped her move back to her seat and buckled her safety belt before getting back behind the wheel and putting his back on. He turned the key in the ignition and, after checking his mirrors, started driving again. "Luke has everyone in this town on high alert to strangers. The people after you are going to have to go through all of us to get to you, Sab."

"That's what I'm afraid of," she muttered under her breath.

Chapter Six

"Fuck," Trent said under his breath when he glanced at his watch and saw how much time had passed by.

Trent was itching to see Sabrina again. It had taken him and Tristan quite a while to get everything on the list, and he hoped that they didn't have to go back to town for anything they'd forgotten. He could see Trick giving orders and sending him and or Tristan back if anything was missing. Not that he'd complain, but he wanted to spend all his free time with their girl. He was itching to kiss her the way Tristan had, and he was pretty sure his big brother would have taken advantage of his alone time with her.

It was really hard to get his brain out of his pants when he'd been walking around with a constant boner since the moment he'd seen Sabrina walk into the diner. He was so horny he was thinking about taking himself in hand, and he hadn't done that for quite a while.

He'd thought that maybe his desires for women had flitted away like the leaves in an afternoon breeze since he hadn't been interested in pursuing the opposite sex for nearly twelve months, but the moment he'd seen Sabrina, he'd known that wasn't the case. As he sat in that diner and stared at her beautiful profile, he'd realized that he was sick of meaningless hookups. He watched the other ménage couples interacting from afar and felt a yearning so deep for what they had his chest had ached. Now that they had her in their lives, there was no chance in hell he was letting her escape.

He wanted the whole nine yards with her and was going to do everything in his power to get her on board. He sighed with relief when Tristan turned the truck into the drive and headed toward the large ranch house in the distance, but when he saw his woman out on the verandah surrounded by the Heritage brothers and laughing, he saw red.

The moment Tristan parked the truck he was out of it and striding toward them. He walked right up to her and grabbed her wrist, spinning her around until she was facing him. "What the fuck do you think you're doing?"

She glared at him and tugged away from his hold. If he hadn't been so damn mad and scared of hurting her, he wouldn't have let her go.

"Take it easy, Trent, it was innocent."

"Stay the fuck away from my woman." Trent scowled at Hank.

Sabrina walked up to him and poked him in the chest with her finger and kept right on poking. From the way her face turned red, he guessed she was just as angry as he felt. "You are a...a...supercilious, patronizing Neanderthal."

The haze of rage over his eyes dissipated, and he looked over at Hank, David, and Barry to see them smirking at him. He lifted his hand and gave them the finger behind her back, but Sabrina took that moment to step sideways and half turn and caught him red-handed.

She slapped a hand onto his chest and shoved him, or tried to, but since she wasn't as tall or as strong as he was, he didn't budge. That just seemed to make her madder. She spun on her heels, making a growling sound in her throat, and stormed away. He couldn't help but do what any red-blooded man would do as he watched her hips twitch and her delectable ass flex as she stomped off down the steps toward the corral.

"You're an idiot, Trent," Barry said before he walked over to the truck to help Tristan unload it.

"Green looks good on you, Wendall," David said with a smirk before he, too, headed to the truck.

"Looks like you have some groveling to do," Hank said. "If I was you I'd stop thinking with my dick and start using the brain in your head."

Trent sighed and scrubbed a hand over his face. He had been an asshole and let his dick and the green-eyed monster rule. He was going to have to eat humble pie and just hoped that Sabrina would accept his apology. With another sigh, he walked off the porch toward the corral. She was looking into the distance and didn't acknowledge his approach.

He stopped right next to her and leaned against the top rail of the corral. "I'm sorry, Sabrina. I don't know what came over me."

She gave him a haughty look, raised an eyebrow at him as if to say, "Really. You expect me to believe that," before turning to watch the horses in the paddock beyond the small arena.

"Okay, so I was jealous. I'm sorry. Will you please forgive me? It won't happen again."

"Do you think I flirt with every man I meet?"

"No."

"Do you think I jump into bed with just anyone?"

"No."

"That's not what it seemed to me by your reaction." She turned to look at him again, and when he saw the hurt in her eyes, he felt like a real bastard.

He reached out clasped her shoulders and turned her toward him. "I'm so sorry for the way I acted and for how I made you feel. It wasn't intentional. I missed you, darlin'. When Tristan and I were out shopping all I could think about was getting back to you as soon as possible. I guess I went off the deep end when I saw you laughing with the Heritage men."

Her eyes softened for a moment, but then they hardened again. "Don't ever treat me like that again, Trent. You made me feel like a hooker."

"You're no such thing, and it never even entered my mind." He tugged her closer and sighed with contentment as her body pressed against his. "I would never do or say anything to intentionally hurt you, darlin'. I was an ass."

"Yes, you were," she said, and even though she was agreeing with him, he thought he heard amusement in her voice.

He drew back slightly and smiled when he saw that she was smirking. "Do you forgive me?"

"Yes."

"Thank you, darlin'." Trent cupped her cheeks in his hands and lowered his head. He rubbed his lips back and forth over hers, hoping she wouldn't shove him away because she was still pissed at him. But she didn't, and he was thankful. She sighed as she melted into him, and then she reached up and gripped his hair.

That was the moment he lost control. He slanted his mouth over hers, kissing her hungrily, passionately, Changing the angle and the fit of their mouths as he pushed his tongue into hers. She tasted so good, so sweet, he wasn't sure he would be able to stop. His hands roamed up and down her body, shaping her curves, learning her secrets, until they landed on her ass and he squeezed her cheeks. He pulled her in tighter against him and thrust his hips into her belly, making her aware of what she did to him. He swallowed her gasp and was about to lift her up when he heard Trick calling him.

With a groan of frustration—but also gratitude because he'd forgotten where he was—he lifted his head to stare at his brother.

"Get over here and help unload the truck."

Trent nodded and eased Sabrina away from him, making sure she was steady on her feet before releasing her. He was glad that Trick had called because he wasn't sure he would have stopped until he'd stripped her naked and was buried inside her pussy. He'd lost total control and hadn't thought about where they were or that there were other people around who may have been watching. That just reiterated to him how special Sabrina was, and he was going to have to be careful about governing his actions with her when others were around. There was no way he wanted anyone but him or his brothers seeing that delectable body naked.

"Why don't you come into the house, darlin'?" He held his hand out to her and waited for her to take it. "Tristan and I bought you some clothes with the help of Damon's wife. He must have seen us coming because she was waiting for us. She picked out everything, as well as selected hair dye and some colored contacts."

She took his hand and let him guide her over to the truck. He removed several bags from the backseat and handed them over to her. "Why don't you go and start sorting through those things and we'll bring in the rest."

"They aren't heavy. I can carry more."

"No, darlin'. Go on. We'll bring the rest." Trent didn't want to load her down with a lot of bags. She was obviously used to doing everything for herself, but she didn't need to anymore. She had him and her brothers to look after her. He didn't care if that sounded chauvinistic, because it wasn't what he meant. He just hoped she would learn to share her problems and let them help her when she needed it. No one could be an island all the time, including him. He had his brothers at his back, but he suspected that Sabrina had had no one. It didn't make her weak to have someone at her side or someone to lean on now and then. Trent just hoped he and his brothers could convince her of that and that they were reliable to have on hand.

But most of all he wanted her love, because he had a feeling he was already well and truly on his way to being in love with her.

* * * *

Sabrina put all the things away after thanking her men for buying her the clothes, and she decided she would make herself useful and cook dinner. She hurried toward the kitchen and saw that Hank, David, and Barry were already busy preparing food.

"Do you want some help?"

"No thanks, honey, we have everything under control. Why don't you just relax?" Hank winked at her and then glanced over at Trent. He was sitting on a stool on the other side of the counter sipping on a beer. Tristan was sitting on the stool beside him. He held out a hand to her, and she walked over to him. He placed his beer bottle on the counter, scooted the seat back, and then lifted her up by the waist before placing her in his lap.

"Do you want something to drink, baby?" Tristan asked as he slipped from the stool. She nodded her head.

"What will you have?"

"There's wine, beer, juice and soda, as well as tea and coffee," David said.

Sabrina picked up Trent's beer and took a sip. She tried to hide her grimace, but when all the men burst out laughing she knew she hadn't been successful. "Do have white wine?"

"Yep," Barry said and reached up to the cupboard above his head for a wineglass.

"Thank you," she said when Tristan placed the wine in front of her.

He smiled, winked, and then leaned over and kissed her on the head. Each time Tristan, Trent, or Trick touched her, hugged her, or kissed her, she fell for them a little more, and although she wanted to accept having a relationship with them, she was scared to. What if she agreed and then those assholes got to them and/or her? It would break her heart if anything happened to them. And even though she'd only just met the Heritage men, she didn't like thinking about them getting hurt either.

She picked up her wineglass and took a sip, savoring the fruity taste of the cool wine as it coated her dry mouth and slid down her throat.

David's voice pulled her from her thoughts.

"It would be better if you stayed out of sight as much as possible, Sabrina. At least until you've had the time to change your appearance. For all any of us know the bastards after you could already be in Slick Rock."

Her heart flipped in her chest, and she drew in a ragged breath.

"We're not trying to scare you, honey, but we all need to be cautious," Hank said before meeting Trick's gaze when he entered the kitchen. "Have you heard anything from Luke or Damon?"

"No." Trick threaded his fingers through his hair. "It will take time for the feds to make their move. They have to do everything by the book or that asshole will be back out on the street before any of us can blink."

"You're right," Tristan said. "I wouldn't put anything past that prick. He has so much money he could probably buy his way out of prison."

"Do you think that will really happen?" Sabrina asked.

"No, darlin'." Trent hugged and adjusted her on his lap. "I don't think Noble will find it easy to get out of this country. He'll have the FBI, CIA, and all the other agencies practically glued to his ass."

"But if he were determined enough he could escape. Right?"

It wouldn't take much for Harvey Noble to change his appearance, and since he was loaded he would no doubt have cash on hand and put it to use. If he managed to leave the US and got into a country that didn't have extradition laws, the asshole would be home free.

She caught Barry nodding from the corner of her eye and turned look at him.

"Yeah. He probably already has a fake identity set up. He would have to know that if anyone found out what he was doing that he'd be in deep shit."

Sabrina gulped down her wine and sighed when languid warmth traveled through her veins as some of the tension eased.

"Try not to worry too much, baby." Trent's hand caressed her upper thigh through her jeans, sending her body into a havoc of need.

Her nipples peaked and began aching, and her pussy clenched as moisture dribbled out of her channel to coat her folds. She shifted on Trent's lap, trying to find a more comfortable position, but she stopped moving when she felt the hard ridge of his cock against her ass cheek and hip.

His hand moved higher on her thigh, and she held her breath for a moment with anticipation and trepidation. He was so close to her pussy, and although she wanted to feel his hand cupping and rubbing her, she didn't want him to move any further. There were other men present, and she didn't want them to see how turned on she was or Trent touching her intimately. She must have tensed, because Trent's hand stopped near the crease of her thigh and hip. She exhaled with relief when he didn't go any higher or over toward her cunt.

She felt his lips on her ear and shivered as his breath caressed her sensitive flesh when he whispered. "No one is going to see me touching you, baby. That's for Trick's, Tristan's, and my eyes only."

When she looked up, it was to see Trick watching her with heated, hungry eyes, but then he blinked and glanced away. She knew she hadn't imagined the passion in his orbs when he met her gaze but was glad he had broken their locked eyes. She didn't want the other men seeing how much she desired the Wendall men. That was private and no one's concern but theirs.

Sabrina was glad when dinner was ready, and Trent lowered her to her feet before guiding her over to the big table. The men talked about the ranch as they ate, and she listened intently, interested in hearing about their horses and beef cattle.

After dinner she tried to help clean up but was again told to rest. She appreciated it for now since she was just getting over the flu, but by tomorrow she hoped to be back to her old self again. There was no way she was going to be idle for the duration of her stay here, even if all she was allowed to do was cook and clean. She needed to feel like she was pulling her weight.

Sabrina had never been idle in her life and wasn't about to start being so now. Everyone adjourned to the large living room, and the men cheered and booed as they watched a rugby game on the TV. Although she stared at the screen, all she could think about was going to bed.

But sleep was the furthest thing from her mind.

Chapter Seven

Sabrina stepped into the bedroom she would be staying in and closed the door. She was tired yet restless and couldn't seem to settle on anything. The men were watching the last minutes of the game, but she wanted to take a shower. Hopefully having the hot water sluicing over her body would help her relax enough to sleep. It wasn't because of the danger she was in that she was feeling restive. It was because her body was one big, massive, needy ache.

She headed to the adjoining bathroom, stripped off her clothes, and turned the shower on. After checking the temperature she stepped in and stood with her eyes closed as the hot water ran over her body. The heat seeped into her muscles and she felt them loosening, and after a couple of minutes, she washed her hair and body before shaving her legs.

After drying off, she wrapped herself up in the thick terry robe Tristan and Trent had bought for her and then brushed out her hair before blowing it dry. Tomorrow she would go from a blonde-haired, blue-eyed woman to having brunette hair and green eyes.

Sabrina hoped that she could get used to having contact lenses and that they didn't irritate her, but she would wear them even if they did. Her life might depend on it.

Just as she came out of the bathroom, someone knocked on her door. She was about to ask who it was, but she didn't really need to. She could practically feel them all standing on the other side of the bedroom door.

She took a deep breath and exhaled nervously before going to the door and opening it. She'd been right. Trick, Tristan, and Trent stood crowded in the hallway.

"Can we come in?" Trick asked, his eyes giving her the once-over before meeting her gaze again.

She gulped nervously and then stood back to let them pass. Trent stopped next to her, removed her clenched hand from the door handle, and closed the door behind him.

"Come and sit down, honey," Tristan said as he patted the space next to where he was sitting on the end of the bed.

She felt Trent's hand on her lower back as he guided her over, and then he sat down on her other side. Trick moved closer, and then he went down to his knees and placed the palms of his hands on her lower thighs right above her knees.

"Do you have any family, Sabrina?" Trick asked.

She shook her head and looked down at his tanned hands. They looked so dark against the white fluffy robe, and she wondered if they would look like that against her skin.

"What happened to your folks, honey?" Tristan asked as he reached for a strand of her hair and rubbed it between his fingers as if he were feeling the texture before bringing it to his nose to sniff it.

"I never had any."

"Shit! That must have been hard on you, baby." Trent took her hand in his and laced their fingers together.

"Yeah, it was. Growing up in an orphanage was no picnic."

"No brothers or sisters, sweetheart?" Trick asked.

"Not that I know of no."

"What about other family?" Trent asked.

"None that I'm aware of," she answered quietly.

"We can be your family," Tristan said as he wrapped an arm around her shoulders and pulled her into his side. Emotion caused her throat to constrict, making it difficult to swallow. She wanted that more than she ever wanted anything in her life, but she couldn't see how having three men could work.

Trick must have seen something in her eyes or face, because he started telling her about ménage relationships. "The men involved in a polyandrous relationship always put their woman first. Her needs and wants are catered to by her men. I've watched all the people in this town involved in those families, and I have to say I have never seen such happy, loving men and women."

"Are they all married?" Sabrina asked, curiosity getting the better of her.

"Yes," Trent answered. "The wife marries the oldest man on paper, but that doesn't mean the others involved aren't treated the same or loved any less. In everyone's heart they are all husbands and wives."

Sabrina nodded, not sure what to say. Her heart yearned for what the other people had, to be loved for who she was, and just the thought of having these three men loving her, touching her, was enough to send her waning arousal back up to a low simmer.

"Sab, we would really like to make love with you." Trick paused to clear his throat, and she felt his fingers twitch on her legs.

She was surprised that such a confident, authoritative man would be nervous around her. When she glanced at Trent and then Tristan, she saw that they both looked tense, too. It was like they were holding their breath. And she realized that she was doing the same when she felt her lungs begin to burn. She exhaled and then inhaled as her heart began to beat fast inside her chest.

"Will you let us show you what being with us would be like, sweetheart?" Tristan almost whispered the question, and she felt his arm flex over her shoulder.

She didn't know if she was making the right decision, all things considered, but she couldn't say no. She wanted to know what it felt like to be with them more than anything, and although she couldn't find her voice to answer, she met each of their gazes before locking her eyes with Trick's and nodding.

She held her breath as Trick got up further onto his knees, and then he was leaning forward. He cupped her face in his hands, keeping their eyes connected until he was too close and out of focus. Her lids lowered, his lips met hers, and she was lost.

She was lost in sensation as his lips moved over then parted hers. His tongue pushed into her mouth, slid along, and then swirled around hers. She breathed him in through her nose, taking his clean masculine scent deep into her lungs, and held him there. But it wasn't only her lungs that were affected. Her heart was, too. Trick, Tristan, and Trent had worked their way under her skin and into her soul. The rightness of this moment was so profound, so poignant, she felt tears of emotion burn the back of her eyes. Her heart was full of joy, and her body was warming up from the inside. The more he kissed her, the more she wanted, and although she knew she would never want to let them go, she couldn't think about that right now.

Trick broke the kiss, and it took all of her ability to not reach out to him when he rose to his feet, but then he was reaching out to her. He took her hands in his and pulled her up from the bed, and as he stared at her for so long she began to wonder if he'd changed his mind.

His next words relieved her mind and made her knees feel weak. "Why don't we get rid of the robe, sweetheart? We want to see all of you." His hands reached for the belt tied at her waist, and he hesitated a moment as if waiting for her to protest, but when she didn't, she felt the knot loosen and then he pushed it from her shoulders.

"Fucking beautiful." She heard Trent's voice as if from a long way off. It felt like she'd been waiting for this moment all her life, and now that it was here—everything felt a little surreal.

"We need to get you more comfortable, baby," Trent whispered in her ear as he moved up behind her, and she gasped when he pulled her back against his front. Her skin felt almost alive, so sensitive, as if all the nerve endings were exposed, as his clothes brushed against her naked flesh. He was so warm and hard, she wanted to turn around and rip his shirt open so she could know what it was like to have his skin beneath her hands and fingertips. But she wasn't that confident and didn't want to do anything wrong.

Trent lifted her up into his arms and then lowered her onto the middle of the bed. He got up on one side of her, and Tristan got up on the other. She looked toward Trick when he pulled his T-shirt up over his head and felt like drooling when she saw his tanned, muscular chest, wide shoulders, large biceps, and washboard abs. Trent and Tristan tugged their shirts off, too, and she panted as she took in their brawny physiques. She'd never seen men as fit and ripped as these three, and just looking at them caused her pussy to clench and drip moisture.

Trick gained the bed near her feet, and she inhaled raggedly when his hands landed on her shins, before caressing up and down over her skin to her lower thighs.

Tristan cupped her cheek and turned her toward him. He'd scooted down on the bed on his side and was lying with his head propped up on his hand. "I need to kiss you again, darlin'."

Then he was doing just that. He didn't start out tentative. He devoured her. And then she moaned into his mouth when a hand cupped and molded one of her breasts. She didn't have to look to know that Trent was touching her. The warmth simmering low in her belly grew hotter and brighter, making her muscles feel like they had no substance. The hands on her legs moved higher and higher, and she couldn't help but arch her hips up, begging for them to touch her where she was aching to be touched.

Her nipple was caressed lightly with a finger or thumb, and then it was being squeezed between the two. The hands on her legs widened them, and her cry was muffled by Tristan's mouth when fingers explored her pussy.

"So fucking wet," she heard Trick rasp.

The mattress between her legs dipped. Arms wrapped around her thighs, and then she was being spread wide. Trent released her mouth just as Trick licked her. The moan which emitted from her lips seemed overly loud in the room, but she couldn't help it.

"Yes, baby," Trent almost growled. "Let us hear how much you like it."

Trick's tongue was gently and slowly laving over her clit. With each pass of his tongue the pleasure grew and the tension built. She moaned when he rimmed a finger around her entrance and then dipped into her creamy cunt. Her pussy clenched, forcing moisture from inside to drip down over her perineum to her ass. But when he pushed that finger up inside, it felt so damn good that her mouth opened on a breathless cry.

Trent took advantage of her gaping mouth and kissed her with a voracious hunger. She couldn't prevent a sob of pleasure when Trick began pumping his finger in and out of her vagina.

"So fucking tight, sweetheart," Trick rasped before he started licking over her clit again. She wanted to reach down, grab hold of his hair, and shove his mouth tighter against her pussy, but she fisted the sheet in her hands instead.

She'd never known the walls of her cunt to be so sensitive before. She felt every slide and glide of his finger as he stroked in and out. Trent's mouth muffled her groan when Trick added another finger. She felt full and stretched, and although everything they were doing to her was blissful, she wanted more.

Trick ramped up the speed of his thrusting fingers as well as the rapid movement of his tongue over her engorged pearl. The fire simmering inside grew, as did the tension in her muscles, and she began to wonder if she would survive such ecstasy.

Tristan leaned down, took a nipple into his mouth, and bit down gently yet firmly, making her cry out, but he didn't hurt her. The pleasure and pain sent another surge of endorphins traveling through her blood, heating it so much she was scared it might start boiling inside her.

Every muscle in her body grew taut, making her arms and legs shake, her stomach muscles jump, and her sheath seemed to gather in on itself.

Trent broke the kiss, and then he, too, was sucking, licking, and biting at her other nipple. Trick did something inside her that caused her to jerk as she hung on the precipice of something so mind blowing that her whole body began to quiver.

And then she was screaming. Her pussy clenched and released around Trick's fingers, only to grab hold before loosening again. She'd never felt anything like she was experiencing in her life as her whole body quaked and quavered in the most monumental orgasm.

She was only vaguely aware of the growls of approval as nirvana buffeted her this way and that. And when she did start to come back down to awareness, she realized that Trick was still lapping lightly at her pussy and she actually heard him swallowing down her juices.

Trent and Tristan were both caressing their hands over her shoulders and arms and sides in slow, soothing strokes while making nonsensical noises. Sabrina hadn't even noticed that her eyes were closed until she opened them, and when she did it was to see three sexy, gorgeous men looking at her as if she'd created the moon and stars.

"I love seeing you come, honey. But the next time you do I am going to be buried inside this pretty little, tight cunt." Trick kissed the top of her mound before he got off the bed. His gaze was still locked with hers as he reached down and opened his jeans and then pushed them and his underwear down.

Her breath stuttered in her throat and her just-satisfied libido began to simmer again when she saw his thick, long cock. She exhaled raggedly and then looked at the ceiling as she tried to get ahold of herself. Her pussy was already clenching and leaking juices in anticipation of being filled, and her blood heated.

She looked back down when she felt the bed dip again, and then Trick was hovering over her. With a quick glance to the sides, she saw that Trent and Tristan had moved away to give their brother room.

His knees were on the bed inside of hers, and his hands were bracketing her near her shoulders. He lowered his head and kissed her lightly on the lips, making her groan with frustration when he didn't deepen it the way she wanted him to, and pulled back again.

"Sabrina, are you a virgin?"

"No," she whispered as heat filled her cheeks. She wished she could have said yes, but she wasn't about to lie.

"When was the last time you had sex, sweetheart?"

Her cheeks heated more, but she was glad that they were getting this out there, because she didn't want them to think she was experienced when it was so far from the truth.

"I had sex in my first year of college and not since."

"Did the guy look out for you?"

"What do you mean?"

"Did he make you come?" Tristan asked.

"No, but it was my first time and I'd heard it could be painful and an orgasm might not happen."

"He was an ass, baby." Trent stroked a finger down her cheek.

Sabrina nodded because she didn't know what to say.

"He hurt you, didn't he?" Trick stated more than asked, and she wondered how the hell he knew that.

She frowned but nodded again.

"How do you know?" she finally managed to ask.

"You got this look on your face right before you climaxed," Tristan said.

"What look?"

"Like you were surprised," Trent answered.

"Umm…"

"I'm glad we could show you a sample of what making love is meant to be like." Trick leaned down and kissed her lips again. "And we have a whole lot more to show you, sweetheart."

Then he was kissing her like she wanted him to. Open mouth, tongue thrusting in and out, and so carnally her body began to burn again.

Sabrina clutched at his shoulders, and he just continued kissing until she thought she would pass out. When he broke the kiss, she gasped in air only to moan as he licked, kissed, and nibbled his way down her neck to her chest.

His lips closed over one nipple, and he suckled on it strongly until she was moving restlessly. He worked his way over to her other nipple and drew on that one firmly, too.

She arched up when his fingers dipped into her soaking pussy, and then he lifted his head to stare into her eyes.

"Are you on the pill, honey?"

She shook her head and hoped they wouldn't have to stop. She mentally cursed herself for not thinking that far ahead.

"Don't go fretting, Sab. I've got you covered." Trick reached over and took a foil packet from Trent. He ripped it open with his teeth, sat back on his heels, and rolled the condom over his cock. "Are you ready for me, honey?"

"Yes," she answered breathily, which made him smile. That smile caused her heart to flip, because it lit up his whole face, making him look even more handsome.

Trick shoved his arms under her legs and then lifted them. His suited cock brushed up and down her folds, making her moan, and then he was pushing inside of her. The wet tissue of her pussy stretched as the head of his cock slid inside. He held still and panted for breath.

"All right, honey?"

"No," Sabrina moaned. "I need more. Give me more, Trick."

"With pleasure, sweetie."

He shoved in a little more and held still again, repeating that process over and over until he was all the way inside. His cock was so thick and long she swore she could feel him in her throat, but it was damn amazing, too.

Sabrina wiggled her hips and bowed up in silent demand and groaned when he heeded her command. He withdrew to the bulbous tip and then slowly shoved back in. With each stroke of his cock in and out of her aching, wet pussy, he increased the pace of his thrusts. His dick glided along her inner walls, faster and faster.

His erection felt stupendous sliding in and out of her cunt, creating a friction so good it almost hurt. Her body began to coil, her muscles becoming stiff as the need inside grew hotter and brighter.

He was moving inside her fast and deep, his pelvis slapping into her ass cheeks, which caused her flesh to ripple and, amazingly, sent more pleasurable vibrations deep inside. She was so close to the peak she could practically taste it, but for some reason she couldn't manage to topple over. Not that it really mattered. She was awed that she was giving Trick pleasure and didn't really care if she didn't get to come a second time.

But all of a sudden Trick shifted up higher onto his knees as he released one of her legs, and then he was gripping an ass cheek with his hand. The changed angle as he shoved down inside her had her sobbing with bliss as his shaft caressed over her clit and the head of his cock touched a very sensitive spot inside.

One stroke, two strokes, and she was screaming. Her pussy contracted hard around his cock as she came. Over and over, her internal walls gripped and let go, and to her surprise, cream gushed from her cunt.

"Fuck yes," Trick growled as he shoved into her again and again. "Come all over me."

Sabrina saw stars as the orgasm seemed to go on and on, and on.

Trick pistoned his cock in and out of her four more times before thrusting forward as deep as he could go, and then he froze inside of her. He roared when his cock twitched and jerked inside her, eliciting more aftershocks as he, too, reached climax. Then he flopped down over her with his weight braced off of her and shoved his head into the crook of her neck.

His breathing was loud in her ear, but she loved hearing it and knowing she was the reason for his breathlessness. She wrapped her arms around his shoulders and held him tight. She loved the feel of his sweat-coated skin beneath her hands and ran them up and down his back, mapping his muscles with her fingertips.

She felt him tense, and then he braced his body and pushed up so he could see her, their lower halves still intimately connected.

"I've never..." He paused to swallow, and she saw so much emotion in his eyes her heart flipped. He leaned down and placed a gentle yet reverent kiss on her lips. "You're amazing, Sab. Special."

Tears filled her eyes, and to her horror, they spilled over.

"Baby, what is it?" Trent asked.

She turned to look at him but couldn't reply because the lump in her throat was too big, so she gave a slight shake of her head.

"Sabrina, did I hurt you?" Trick asked.

"No," she managed to say even if her voice was a little husky. "You made me feel so much."

Trick smiled and winked, and then they both groaned as he pulled his cock from her body.

"I know just how you feel, honey," he said before rolling off the bed and heading toward the bathroom.

She couldn't help but watch and drool over his sexy ass flexing as he walked away.

Chapter Eight

Trent couldn't wait any longer. He needed Sabrina, and he needed her now. He rolled from the bed and tugged at the button of his jeans so hard it went flying across to the other side of the room and hit the wall. He didn't care. All he cared about was sinking into her hot, wet pussy.

He shoved his jeans and boxers down and cursed under his breath when he realized he still had his boots on. He toed his boots off, and then he kicked his jeans and boxers aside. He took a deep breath and closed his eyes a moment as he tried to get his raging hunger under control and was pleased he did, otherwise he might have done the unthinkable and joined with Sabrina without getting a condom. He rushed over to the bedside table, tore the pack open, and rolled it down his cock as he got up onto the bed beside her.

He barely glanced at Trick when he came back from the bathroom and took a seat on the sofa across the room.

Trent needed to make sure she was with him all the way before he even thought about pushing into her body. He lay down beside her, and when she turned her head to look at him, he reached up, cupped her cheeks, and slanted his mouth over hers. He kissed her like there was no tomorrow, and right now there wasn't. There was only the here and now with her.

He growled into her mouth when he felt her fingers threading through his hair and shifted his hands down to position her onto her side before pulling her up against him. He groaned when her warm, soft, naked skin connected with his, the sensation so intense his eyes burned.

He mapped her curves with his hands, still kissing her hungrily, and shifted his body away from hers slightly so he could cup her breasts. His hands molded her soft, plump globes, and she arched them further into his hands while making a kittenish mewing sound in the back of her throat.

Fuck! I love those sexy little sounds she makes. I want to hear more.

Trent strummed his thumbs back and forth over her nipples as he thrust his tongue into her mouth, dancing with and along hers. She tasted so fucking sweet, so right, he wanted to kiss her forever. But he couldn't because he needed to fill his lungs with more air, and he had no doubt that she did, too, so he slowed the kiss and then gasped in a breath before he nibbled down her neck. He smiled against her skin when he felt her shiver when he found a sweet spot, so he sucked the skin into his mouth and nipped it.

She moaned, and then her hands were on his chest, caressing over his pecs before moving out to his biceps, up to his shoulders, and back down again. He moaned when her soft little hands moved passed his pectoral muscles to his torso and down to his hard abs.

Trent didn't want her going any lower. Not because he didn't want her to or love the way she touched him, but because he was so turned on he just might shoot off before her even got inside of her. He wrapped his hands around her wrists and pulled them away from his body as he lifted his head to meet her gaze.

"I love the way you touch me, baby, but I'm too triggered right now." He placed her hands onto his shoulders, and then he began touching her again. He pinched a nipple between his thumb and finger while the other hand cupped her mound. Trent met Tristan's eyes and saw the hunger burning in his brother's gaze. "Lift her leg up."

Tristan nodded and did as he asked, and then Trent delved into her humid heat. He tested to make sure she was ready, and when he found she was, he scooted forward, aligned his cock with her pussy, and pushed in.

He swore he felt his eyes roll back in his head as her wet heat enveloped the head of his dick, and the urge to shove in was nearly too much for him to stop. But he did, because there was no way in hell he wanted to hurt her.

Sabrina must have felt as eager as he did, thank god, because she was the one to undulate her hips toward him, taking more of his cock into her pussy. "Jesus, baby. So fucking good."

"Yes," she gasped before she started rocking her hips back and forth, taking more and more of him inside of her.

Trent needed more, but he liked that she was controlling how much she took of him and decided to give her free reign. "Let her go," he told Tristan, and when his brother had released her leg, he rolled onto his back, taking her with him.

"Oh," Sabrina gasped, and he looked down to see that her knee was in danger of slipping off the edge of the mattress, so he scooted them both toward the middle.

"Better?"

"Yes."

"Good. I want you to ride me, baby. Take what you need."

She hummed as her eyes slid closed and she pushed down onto him.

Trent ground his teeth and hoped like hell he could hold out until she found her pleasure before taking his own.

She moved her hands from his shoulders to his pecs and pushed up until she was sitting above him. And then she started moving. She was so fucking sexy as she rocked back and forth and then up and down on his cock, her hips swaying and undulating like he imagined a belly dancer's would. The walls of her pussy rippled and moved over and around his dick as she rode him.

With each motion, she sped up and her ass cheeks slapped against his balls and thighs. Tingling heat formed at the base of his spine, and he wasn't sure how much longer he could hold out. He nodded at Tristan and nearly chuckled at his brother's eagerness.

Tristan quickly crawled around behind her, and Trent didn't have to ask what his brother had done when she squealed and froze.

"Wh–what are you doing?"

"I'm just exploring and trying to make you feel good, darlin'."

"What's he doing, baby?"

"Umm..." Sabrina nibbled on her lower lip, looking uncertain. "He's touching my...my bottom."

"Do you like it?" Trent asked and held his breath while he waited for a reply.

"It's...different."

"Come here, baby." Trent tugged her down and slanted his mouth over hers. He wanted to keep her distracted while Tristan played with her ass. He heard the *pop* of a bottle and knew his brother had just grabbed the lube.

When Sabrina's cunt clenched around his dick and she moaned into his mouth, he knew Tristan was massaging the gel into her anus. She was the one to break the kiss this time, and she pushed up onto her forearms while staring at him through heavy-lidded, passion-glazed eyes.

He was about to ask her to tell him what Tristan was doing again, but her mouth opened on a moan and her eyes closed. Her cheeks were flushed with desire, and when he looked down he saw that the blush went all the way down to her breasts. He lifted a hand from her hip before taking her breast into it and kneading it.

"So fucking tight," Tristan rasped before looking up and meeting his gaze. "She's gonna need to be stretched some."

Trent wanted to give Tristan the time to play with her some more, but he couldn't hold out anymore. Her cunt hadn't stopped rippling around his hard dick from the moment he'd entered her, and even though the tingling at the base of his spine had dissipated, he was aching to the point of pain.

He released her breast, gripped her hips again, and lifted her up before pulling her back down. She mewled right before she started rocking faster before changing to rising up and down on his cock.

"Damn, honey. Good girl," Tristan panted out between breaths. "You're taking two fingers now."

The tingling was back, but this time it didn't start off slow and build up. It covered the whole base of his spine and swept around to his balls. They heated, hardened, and drew up as she moved up and down on his dick faster and faster, harder, taking him deeper. Just when he thought he would lose it before she would, he felt her break first. She clenched on him hard, a soft scream emitting from between her lips as she shook and shuddered over and around him.

That was it for Trent.

He shoved up into her hard and fast twice more, a roar spewing from his mouth the same time cum spewed up his cock and out into the tip of the condom. His vision wavered, and even though he kept his eyes open and his gaze on her face, it looked like he was seeing her through a thick fog.

His balls ached from the force of his sperm roiling and shooting up his cock, and he came like he'd never come before, until he wasn't certain if he would stay conscious. The fog had gone, but only because his vision was now a dark blackness, leaving him blind.

When he came back down, he loosened his tight hold on Sabrina's hips and hoped he hadn't hurt or marked her. She was slumped down over him, breathing heavily but totally relaxed.

"She's going to be heaven to fuck in the ass," Tristan said, and she moaned when Trent withdrew his fingers from her anus.

"Not just the ass," Trent said when he could finally talk. "Our woman is mind-blowing to make love with." He kissed the top of her head. "You okay, baby?"

"Hmm."

"Are you up for some more loving, darlin'?" Tristan asked.

"Hmm."

"Looks like your mind wasn't the only one blown," Trick said with a chuckle.

Sabrina giggled.

Trent rolled them both to their sides and eased his deflating cock from her pussy. He was about to head to the bathroom and deal with the condom, but when she whimpered he froze. He cupped her face in her hands. "Look at me, Sab."

Her eyes opened and met his. "Are you tender, baby?"

"No."

He gave her a hard stare, and she sighed before saying, "I'm a little tender but nothing to worry about."

"I'm sorry if I was too rough with you, Sabrina."

She reached out and touched his cheek. "You weren't. I'm not used to this, remember?"

"Why don't you go have a shower or bath, darlin'?" Tristan suggested as he moved back to her other side.

Trent met his eyes and saw the disappointment on his brother's face, but their woman's comfort and needs were theirs to take care of, and if she was too sore, Tristan was going to have to wait.

"I don't want a bath. At least not yet." She rolled over to face Tristan. "I want you, Tristan. Will you make love to me?"

"I don't want to hurt you, darlin'. I think we should wait."

Sabrina sat up and glanced over the bed. She got to her hands and knees before reaching over to the bedside table and grabbing the bottle of lube. She waved it in the air. "I think this should take care of things."

"Sabrina, don't feel you have to—" Tristan didn't get to finish his sentence because Sabrina placed a finger over his lips.

"I want you to make love to me, Tristan. Please?"

"How can I refuse you, darlin'? But please tell me to stop if I hurt you or you're too sore. Okay?"

"Yes."

"Stay on your hands and knees for me, Sabrina."

Trent got off the bed and went to clean up. His brother was trying to hide how hungry he was for their girl, but there was no hiding anything from him and Trick. They knew each other too well.

* * * *

Tristan got off the bed, walked to the bottom of it, and then reached for Sabrina. He clasped her hips in his hands and pulled her toward him until her knees were on the edge of the mattress. He ripped open the condom pack, rolled the prophylactic on, and then took the lube from her hand. She looked back at him over her shoulder and waggled her ass at him. He couldn't resist and slapped her on one cheek and then the other. She sighed, spread her legs wider, and lowered her shoulders to the bed.

He opened the lube and squirted a generous dollop onto his suited cock before spreading it and then squeezed out more onto two fingertips. He rimmed the entrance to her pussy before pushing those fingers up inside to disperse the cool gel and was pleased when she moaned. But in this position he couldn't see her face, and he needed to know he wasn't hurting her.

Since Trent was still in the bathroom, he looked back at Trick. "I need you to watch her."

Trick nodded, stood, and walked over to the bed before lying across it near Sabrina's head. He met Tristan's gaze, smiled, and nodded. Relief surged through him that he wasn't making her uncomfortable. He pumped his fingers in and out of her a few times but kept a watch on his brother in case he needed to stop, and was glad that Trick hadn't given him a signal to do so.

After withdrawing his fingers from her cunt, he grabbed the base of his dick, aligning it with her pussy, and then he was pushing inside her. Her wet, tight heat felt like pure heaven, and as he pushed in a little more, he realized he was shaking. Shaking from desire but also from the need to keep in control. When she pushed back onto him with a moan he cursed and gripped her hips a little firmer, but having her hot, wet cunt enveloping him was too sweet and his control shattered.

With a growl of hunger, of a need he'd never felt before, he withdrew slightly and then surged in deep. He held still and glanced at Trick when she whimpered and then sighed with relief when his brother gave him the thumbs-up before he shifted under her near her breasts. Her pussy clenched around his cock, and he could hear the slurping sounds Trick made as he sucked one of her buds before releasing it and moving over to the other.

Tristan's shaking grew more intense, and he couldn't hold still another moment. He tightened his fingers on her hips, drew back, and then drove into her. The pace he set was fast, hard, and deep.

With each pump forward she moaned and tried to push back against him, but he was too close to allow her any leeway. He needed to keep her still or he was going to blow way too soon. Trick moved out from under Sabrina but continued to pluck at her nipples with his fingers.

He wrapped an arm around her hips as he continued to pump his own, sliding his cock in and out of her tight, moist grip. When he felt the tingling begin at the base of his spine, he knew he was close to being done for, so he used his free hand and searched out her clit. At first he drew light circles over and around it, but when the heat increased and started moving toward his balls, he thrummed it faster with a firmer touch.

Sabrina was gasping and groaning each time he stroked into her, and the more pleasure he gave her, the wetter and hotter she got. The ripples of her inner walls grew closer together, and he knew she wasn't far away from coming. Sweat beaded on his forehead, and his muscles were so pumped they felt harder than they'd ever been. He could actually feel the cum roiling in his balls as they drew up, ready for release.

Tristan pinched her clit firmly between his finger and thumb, and she screamed. Her whole body tensed just before her cunt clamped down onto his cock then released and clamped down again. He shoved through her contracting cunt twice more and then yelled as his balls drew up further and fire raced through his whole body as he came like he'd never come before.

His body shuddered and juddered with bliss, and he saw stars before his eyes. Cum shot up to the tip of his cock and spewed out with the most glorious pressure and nirvana he'd ever felt. It was the longest climax he'd ever experienced, and he hoped he didn't pass out only to fall on top of Sabrina and crush her.

How long it took before he came back down from the stars, he had no idea, but was glad he hadn't flattened her into the mattress when he found some of his equilibrium again. His body was curved over hers, but he was still braced on his arms and knees. Sabrina's head and shoulders were on the bed with her face turned to the side as she gasped for air. The satisfied smile that crossed her lips filled him with a masculine power, but he was also filled with a possessiveness he'd never felt before.

Tristan wrapped his arms around her tight and breathed in their combined scents. She smelt right, she felt right, and he was going to convince her with his brothers' help that she was right for all of them.

Yes, he had been covetous of her when he'd first seen her and known she was the one for him and his brothers, but this was so much more than he'd first thought. His heart felt like it would burst open at any moment, and the thought of another man touching her filled him with jealousy. But the thought of her being in danger filled him with rage.

Tristan was so in love with her, and he wasn't about to let anyone near her. It was up to him, his brothers, the Heritage men, and the other men in town to make sure she was safe. Even if it meant taking a bullet or killing for her.

Nothing else was acceptable.

Chapter Nine

"Fucking bastard," Sawyer cursed Noble under his breath. The fucker was safely holed up in a rundown motel in Fort Collins waiting for a call from him to tell him he had taken out his ex-personal assistant. The bastard thought he was safe hiding in Fort Collins since he had false papers and had attempted to change his appearance. That wouldn't help him with agents looking for the prick. He couldn't change his features, and since he was ugly he stood out like a sore thumb. Just one look at the bastard's nose and the feds would know him without having to look at any pictures. Harvey liked to drink whiskey, and because of that, his large nose was always red. No, the law would have no trouble pegging him.

What Noble didn't know was that Sawyer wasn't about to become the asshole's scapegoat. He didn't trust that fucker not to turn him in to try and save his own ass. Noble thought he was stupid, but he was far from it. He knew if the shit hit the fan that he would end up having to take Harvey down so he could make a run for it. He knew all about the money in the trunk of the rental that prick had leased, and he was going to make damn sure he got his hands on that cash and skipped out if things went south. He didn't have any qualms about putting a bullet in Noble's head for self-preservation.

His eyes glanced around the dimly lit room from beneath his eyelashes, taking in the people. He had entered Slick Rock last night, and although he made sure to keep a low profile, he felt like he was constantly being watched. It was pretty hard trying to make himself look nonthreatening when he was six foot two and full of muscle, but he had learned to walk with his shoulders hunched, his head down, and to keep eye contact to a minimum, but for some reason it wasn't working here. He caught people watching him from his periphery and under his lowered lashes, but what bothered him was that they weren't worried about making it known that he was being observed.

He decided that it might be prudent to leave town and head to one close-by and come back at night after renting a different car to do some reconnoitering. As he sat in the back of the bar and ate his dinner, with his back to the wall, of course, he glanced up and saw two sheriffs still in uniform looking around. He was damn glad he had several sets of false papers and hoped that the two lawmen walking toward him would believe he was a tourist just passing through. He doubted it, but it was worth a try. The men came closer and sat in the two chairs opposite him without waiting for an invitation.

"Howdy. Nice little town you have here," Sawyer said with a smile that no doubt didn't reach his eyes.

"Where are you from?" the tan-skinned man asked.

"New York," Sawyer replied.

"You don't sound like you're from there," the other sheriff said as he leaned back in his seat and crossed his arms over his chest.

Sawyer realized then that these two men weren't slow, country-town, hick sheriffs and he would need to keep his wits about him. "No, you're right. I grew up in Denver but moved to the city when I finished college. I'm a salesman and had to be in Cortez for work."

"So you're just passing through?" the other one asked.

"Yes, sir. I'll be leaving at first light if not before. I'm stopping in Denver to see the folks before getting the red-eye back to New York."

"Got any ID on you?"

"Sure do," Sawyer replied as he pulled his wallet from his pocket, removed the fake license, and handed it over.

The bronze-skinned sheriff studied his ID intently before handing it back. "Drive carefully, Mr. Boseman." Both of the men rose to their feet before sauntering over to the bar to speak to the bartender.

Sawyer finished his dinner in a timely manner without rushing and ordered another beer. The sheriffs left not long after, and even though he didn't catch the bartender watching him, he knew he was. By the time he left the hotel and walked back to the motel, the hair on the back of his neck was standing on end.

He was glad he'd decided to move out first thing because he had a feeling he hadn't been able to put anything over the sheriffs or the bartender. In fact, he felt like he had turned from predator to prey, and he didn't like that feeling. Not one little bit.

* * * *

It had been a week since Sabrina and the Wendall brothers had arrived at the Heritage Ranch, and even though she loved spending time with her men and the Heritages, she knew deep down that something was going to happen to destroy the newfound happiness she was feeling.

She went through each day laughing and joking, but there was the niggling fear deep down inside that never left. She was currently in the kitchen with Tristan making sandwiches for when the men came back inside from doing their chores. Trent and Trick were out there helping, and although she worried about them all being out in the open where they could get hurt, there was nothing she could do to stop them. She'd tried each and every day to keep the Wendall brothers inside with her, but they just smiled at her, stroked her cheek, hugged or kissed her, and went about their merry way.

She looked up to see Tristan watching her with a concerned frown on his face.

"What?" she asked as she went back to making the sandwiches.

"I don't know. Why don't you tell me?" Tristan asked as he moved in behind her and hugged her around the waist.

"I'm worried." She sighed and leaned back against him for a moment before straightening up as she began to put the food onto a large platter. The table was already set with plates, mugs, and glasses, and iced tea was in a jug chilling in the fridge. There was also a large fresh pot of coffee brewing.

"I can see that, darlin', but what about?"

"You all go outside every day and are in plain view. What if this person has a scope and long-range rifle and shoots you?" A small sob escaped as she placed the last sandwich on the plate.

Tristan turned her around in his arms, pulled her against him, and held her tight. "Sabrina, there is no way this bastard can find you. No one in town is going to give away your hiding place."

"I know, but…I can't lose you, Tristan. Any of you. I love you all so damn much. How am I going to live with my conscience if something happens to one or all of you?" Tears spilled from her eyes and onto her cheeks. The pain in her chest at the thought of losing any of her men was almost too much to bear.

Tristan hugged her tighter, resting his head on top of hers. She breathed in his spicy masculine scent and savored being in his arms. When she heard the back door slam, she tried to pull away, but he wouldn't let her. She quickly wiped the moisture from her face and took a deep breath, trying to calm her worries.

"Is everything all right?" Hank asked as he came into the kitchen.

"Yes." Sabrina pulled away again and was glad when Tristan let her. She looked toward the door to see all the men entering, and then Trick and Trent came over to her.

"You okay, sweetheart?" Trick asked as he stroked a hand over her head.

Sabrina gulped around the lump in her throat and nodded before turning away to pick up the platter and carry it to the table.

The men talked about the ranch while they devoured their lunch, and if Sabrina had been in a better frame of mind she may have teased and laughed with them over the amount of food they all put away, but she was feeling down and couldn't seem to find any lighthearted optimism.

She knew it wouldn't take long for Noble's crony or cronies to find her. Both the sheriffs took turns coming out to keep them updated and checking in on things, and it would be easy for those assholes to follow them.

Sabrina was sure that they were vigilant in making sure they weren't followed, but Noble was a computer and gadget expert and it would be simple enough to bug the vehicles and track them. She had a target painted on her forehead, and there was not a damn thing she could do about it.

No. That's not true. I can leave. If I leave then they will all be safe.

Her mind whirled as she tried to plan how to get away without being seen. It was going to be damn hard when she was never alone. But she was smart, and if she used her head she would find a way to make that happen without being discovered.

"Sabrina, do you want to go for a horse ride this afternoon?" Trick asked.

"We know you've been getting cabin fever," Trent said.

"I've never been on a horse."

"You don't have to worry about that, honey," Hank said with a smile. "We have a very gentle mare that is perfect for beginners."

Tristan reached over and clasped her hand. "You'll be safe, darlin'. We'll all go along for the ride and we'll take rifles with us."

It was too tempting to pass up. Sabrina had been going insane staying inside all the time. It would be good to get out into the fresh, clean air and let her worries stew on the back burner for a while.

"If you think it's safe, then I would love to go for a ride."

"Go and get some jeans on, baby," Trent said. "We'll clean up while you get ready."

Sabrina nodded, got up, and left the room. She was wearing a skirt and shirt and knew she couldn't ride a horse in them. By the time she walked back to the living room, Trent was the only one left inside waiting for her.

He moved toward her and pulled her into his arms before hugging her. "You've been pretty quiet the last couple of days. What's bugging you, baby?"

"I'm just worried that whoever is after me will find me and hurt all of you. It would be easy to follow the sheriffs out here or to bug their vehicles with tracking equipment."

Trent pulled back and nudged her chin up. "Sabrina, Damon is a retired Marine. He and Luke weren't born yesterday. They've been very vigilant to make sure they weren't followed out here when they come. And yes, they've even been going over their vehicles to make sure it's safe."

"Have they found anything?"

The expression which crossed Trent's face answered her question. Fear slammed into her hard and fast, making it difficult to breathe. Her heart hammered in her chest, and she began to shake as light perspiration formed on her skin.

"They have, haven't they?" she asked in a shaky whisper.

Trent tugged her up against him again and caressed his hand up and down her back. "Take a deep breath for me, Sab."

She did and then exhaled noisily.

"Good girl. Keep breathing. Everything is going to be fine. Nothing is going to happen to you, baby. Not if we can help it."

"That's just it, Trent. I don't want you, your brothers, or the Heritage men getting—"

"Shh." Trent held her tighter, continually stroking her back in a soothing motion. "I love you, Sabrina, so do my brothers. We aren't about to let anyone take you from us. Not when we've just found you."

"You can't make those types of promises, Trent. You don't know what's going to happen," she sobbed.

"Neither do you, baby. Why borrow trouble when it isn't here yet?"

"It's coming, Trent. I can feel it to my bones." A sob escaped.

"This town is full of men who are strong. There is a lot of retired military, and the ranchers know how to handle themselves. We have all their phone numbers programmed into our cells. All it would take is one phone call and nearly every man would be here with guns blazing. You're not going to run, Sabrina. We'll only follow you if you do. You're safer here than anywhere else."

Sabrina rested her forehead against his chest and nodded. She knew he was right, but she was still worried about all their safety. She withdrew a smidgeon and then reached up and cupped his cheeks in the palm of his hands. "I love you, too, Trent."

"Thank God," Trent whispered before he bent down and started kissing her. The kiss started off slow but quickly turned wild and passionate. By the time he drew back, they were both breathing heavily.

"Damn, baby, you pack quite a wallop." He grinned and then adjusted the front of his jeans. "If we don't get out of here right now, I'm going to carry you to bed."

Trent took her hand in his and led her out toward the barn. "It's going to be damned uncomfortable trying to ride with a boner," he muttered and then winked at her.

Sabrina burst out laughing. She could just imagine how hard it would be—pun intended. It felt good to laugh again, and as she was lifted up onto the mare by Trick, she prayed that Noble and his cronies were caught before anyone could get hurt.

"How much land do you own?" Sabrina asked Barry, who was riding on the other side of Trick. She was sandwiched between Trick and Tristan with Hank leading the way and David bringing up the rear with Trent. She felt safe since she was surrounded on all sides, and for the first time in the last few days, she really relaxed. It was so nice to be outside in the crisp, cool autumn air after being locked up in the house as she recovered from the flu. She was feeling better than ever and could have spent hours out in the sunshine.

"We have over ten thousand acres. Our dads bought the land before they met our mom and had started building the house."

"How many fathers do you have?" Sabrina asked curiously. This town was so out of the norm with the polyandrous relationships, but no one seemed to bat an eye at the unusual. At first she'd been a little shocked, but after Trick, Trent, and Tristan had explained how things worked and told her how happy everyone was, she accepted that this town didn't conform to normality. Not that any of it bothered her at all. She'd always been a live-and-let-live person as long as everyone agreed and was happy.

"Two," Hank said and smiled at her. "My mom needs the both of them to keep up with her. She has always been full of life and energy. She loved this place, but as the folks got older and she could see that our dads were slowing down she suggested that my brothers and I could take over for them so they could retire to warmer climes."

"She must be an amazing person."

"She is."

"Maybe I'll get to meet her one day," Sabrina said.

"She'd love you, honey," Hank said as he turned to face her. "She has been on our backs about meeting someone to settle down with." He winked at her before continuing on, and she wondered what he was up to when she saw the twinkle in his eye. "You'd be right up her alley for a daughter-in-law."

"Hey, Sabrina's taken," Trick said in a playful growly voice. "Get your own damn woman."

"Do you have any friends, sugar?" Barry asked in a louder voice from behind her.

"Yeah. I was sharing a house with Nicole. Maybe I'll be able to get her out here for a visit one day." She glanced over at Trick. "Do you think it would be safe to call her? I feel really bad for leaving the way I did. I called from a pay phone and told her to lease my room since I had to leave for a family emergency."

"I don't think that's a good idea, honey," Trick answered. "Noble probably has her phone tapped."

"I feel so bad about leaving the way I did and without any notice." Sabrina stared off into the distance and hoped that Nicole was safe and had been able to find another roommate.

"You did what you had to, darlin'." Tristan reached over and squeezed her hand before releasing it again.

"I know." She sighed. "But that doesn't make me feel any less guilty."

"I'm sure she'll understand once you tell her why you did what you did after all this is over," Trick said.

"I hope so."

The afternoon went by quickly. They didn't spend too long riding since it was her first time out, and before she knew it they were heading back to the house.

"You don't want to spend too long in the saddle your first time. Your muscles aren't used to it and will stiffen up," Hank explained just as the house came into view.

Sabrina nodded, and even though she felt like she could have kept riding, she let the experienced ranchers guide her since she was a novice. Trick dismounted and then lifted her down to the ground. She thanked the Heritage men and turned toward the house. She was going to wash up and then get supper ready. It was the least she could do since she was disrupting everyone's lives.

Trick followed her up to the house, and just as they stepped through the door his cell phone rang. He pulled his phone from his pocket and walked back out onto the porch. Sabrina continued on to the bathroom.

She had that bad feeling back in her gut and hoped that the phone call was one of the sheriffs calling to tell Trick that Noble had been caught, but she knew that was wishful thinking. Nothing had been that easy so far.

How long is it going to be before I can live without fear?

Chapter Ten

He glanced at his watch and saw that it was still just over an hour before dinner preparations would need to start and decided this would be a perfect time to spend some alone time with his woman. He looked toward the barn and saw that his brothers and the Heritage men were rubbing down the horses. Hopefully they would be at it for a while because he needed to be with Sabrina.

"I need to feel her in my arms," he muttered under his breath as he stared at the back door.

Trick pondered on whether to tell Sabrina about Noble being arrested, but he didn't think that was such a great idea right now. She was more relaxed than he'd ever seen her after enjoying an afternoon ride in the cool fresh air. Plus there wasn't anything she could do right now. What frustrated him the most was that neither could he or his brothers. The only thing they could do was continue to make sure she was safe. Luke had told him not to let their guard down, because even though Noble was in jail awaiting trial, his cohorts were still out on the loose. Until the law got all the information from Noble, they would have to stay vigilant.

He loved her so damn much, and it irked him no end that he couldn't do anything other than protect her. He wished he knew who was after her, because if he did, he wouldn't be waiting for that fucker to make his move. No, he would use all his resources with the help of the other men in town and hunt that bastard down. He could just imagine Luke reading him the riot act, but he knew his lawman friend wouldn't hold a grudge for long. All he would need to do is point out that he would do the same thing if his wife was in danger. Of course he would do everything he could to make sure he didn't kill the prick, but if worst came to worst, he would do it in a heartbeat. Especially when it meant that Sabrina would be safe.

He pushed his phone back into his pocket and headed inside. After checking the kitchen and living room and finding no Sabrina, he walked toward the bedroom. She wasn't in there either, but he heard water running. Perfect. He was sure he needed a shower, too, after spending time on a horse.

Without any hesitation, he stripped off and quietly opened the bathroom door. She took his breath away. Her eyes were closed, her head tilted back, and she sighed as water sluiced down her body. And what a body it was. She wasn't tall, but she was curvy with full, round, perky breasts, hard rosy-brown nipples, and slender hips and legs. His cock twitched and started filling with blood. He was so in love with her he wanted to stay buried inside her for all time, but it wasn't just about the sex. Although that was damn explosive between them. He'd never been with such a responsive, passionate woman, and he craved her all the time. No, it wasn't just lust. She got to him like no other woman ever had or ever would. She'd grabbed hold of his heart, and he never wanted her to let go.

Trick was still a little worried that she would decide to try and take off, but he and his brothers hadn't given her a chance. One of them had been with her throughout each and every day and would continue to do so. He also wanted to ask her to marry him and his brothers, but he didn't think now was the right time. Not with her life still in danger. He could just imagine her hedging before changing the subject without answering, and since he wasn't sure he could handle any rejection from her, he was going to wait. When this shit was all over, then it would be time to make sure she was in their lives for all time.

Trick pushed his thoughts aside, opened the shower door, and stepped in behind her. She must have felt the cooler air as the door closed or felt his presence, because her eyes popped open and she gasped, her hand going to her chest.

"Sorry, honey. I didn't mean to scare you."

"You didn't, not really. More like startled me. What are you doing?"

He grinned at her as he snagged an arm around her waist, pulling her delectable body against his as he waggled his eyebrows in carnal suggestion. "Taking a shower."

"And you couldn't wait until I'd finished?" she asked breathlessly.

"Nope. I need you, sweetheart." Trick thrust his hips, pushing his hard cock into her stomach, and was pleased when her eyelids drooped and her saw the passion begin to smolder.

When her lips parted he couldn't wait another minute. She started to say something, but he captured her lips with his and thrust his tongue into her mouth. Her hands came up to grip his shoulders and she moaned with desire as she kissed him back. The kiss was hot, wet, and wild, and his cock started pulsing with his heartbeat and his need for her. He was so damn randy he needed her now.

He broke the kiss and licked his way down her neck toward her breasts, and then he drew a nipple into his mouth and suckled firmly. She started rocking her hips and mewled before her one of her hands caressed down his chest and lower. He was the one groaning next, when her small, delicate, soft, little hand gripped his hard cock. He let her pump his shaft a few times, but he was so eager for her he couldn't take much more. He clasped her wrist and tugged her hand away from his erection before switching to suck her other nipple. She moaned when he slid his fingers through her folds and around her cunt to make sure she was ready for him. He growled low in his throat when he found her dripping wet.

He released her nipple with a soft pop and then her lifted her up and pressed her back against the tile wall. She was with him every step of the way, and she slung her arms around his neck and hooked her legs around his hips. He stared deeply into her eyes as he drew his pelvis back slightly until his cockhead was at her entrance and began to push into her, and her eyes began to close.

"Keep your eyes on me, honey," he demanded breathlessly as he eased all the way into her. He groaned at her tight grip on him, and he was the one struggling to keep his eyes open, but he needed to watch her as he loved her. Needed to see every expression of her passion as he loved her.

He started rocking his hips, sliding his cock in and out of her wet pussy as they both panted for breath. With each thrust he increased the pace and depth until their bodies were slapping together and making sucking sounds as the water sluiced between them. Her sheath rippled around him with each stroke, and too fast, the base of his spine began to tingle. He wanted to spend hour upon hour loving her, but right now, with them connected intimately and her face tinged pink with passion as he stared into her beautiful eyes, he was quickly losing control.

The love he could see in her gorgeous orbs went straight to his heart, and he was so full of emotion he didn't know if he could contain it. She was so right for him and his brothers he couldn't bear the thought of not having her in his life.

Trick moved his hands from her hips down to her ass and gripped her cheeks. He spread them wide, bent his knees a little more, and started plunging into her faster. The head of his dick bumped against her cervix, and when she moaned louder he knew she liked it. He pulled her tighter into him, making sure the shaft of his cock rubbed against her clit, and started stroking into her like a man possessed. And he was with her, the love of his life.

Sabrina moaned and gasped as her nails dug into his back, and he knew she was getting close. That was a damn good thing because the heat at his lower back was moving around to his balls and cock.

Her internal muscles got tighter and started rippling around his dick, and she started keening softly. All the while he loved her, their eyes stayed connected. When hers glazed over and her mouth opened a little more, he reached out with a finger and massaged her anus. Her nails dug deeper, and then she was screaming softly, her eyes unfocused as her cunt gripped and rippled around his shuttling cock, covering him in her cum.

That was all it took to send him over with her.

He shoved into her once more and froze, giving a short yell as his balls turned hard as stone when they drew up close to his body and fire shot up his shaft as he came. Each time he ejaculated, her pussy clenched around him, drawing out everything he had to give and maybe a little more. By the time they'd finished coming together, he felt like he'd poured his heart and soul into her and his balls were tender from the force of his climax. His legs were shaking, and he was breathing like he'd just run the hundred-yard dash.

Trick leaned forward and kissed her. It was a passionate kiss, but it was also a kiss to show and tell her how much he loved her. He intended to spend the rest of his life showing and telling her each and every day just how much she meant to him when the danger was over.

* * * *

Sab was pleased to hear that Damon, his brothers, and their wife were coming out for a visit. They'd already had dinner, and she was in the process of cleaning up with Tristan and Trent's help.

She was happy with how much the men had liked her dinner of pot roast and how much they had eaten. Each of them had complimented her on her cooking, and after such praise and a relaxing ride in the cool afternoon air, she was feeling pleasantly mellow and tired for a change. Plus, Trick had made love to her in the shower. By the time he'd finished with her she'd felt like a pile of insubstantial goo.

But she still couldn't help being scared that something bad was going to happen.

She was sick of feeling tense all the time and looked forward to meeting Damon's brothers, Sam and Tyson, and their wife, Rachel. She would love to meet all the other women and men who were involved in ménage marriages, but she couldn't see that happening until this thing with Noble was over.

The Heritage men, as well as Trick, Trent, and Tristan, had told her about all the people in town and how happy they were. Maybe when this was finished and she was free to live her life she would organize a BBQ for everyone. She figured it was the least she could do after what everyone was doing to try to protect her.

She heard a knock on the door as the last of the dishes were put away and the counters wiped down. As she reached for the coffee to make a fresh pot, Tristan reached out and clasped her wrist.

"Why don't you let Trent and I do that, darlin'? You're looking a little weary."

"I'm fine."

Tristan tugged her wrist, and she bumped into him as she lost her balance. She sighed when his arms wrapped around her waist and pulled her in tighter against him. She inhaled deeply, loving the way he and his brothers always smelled so damn good. Her libido chose that moment to light up. It didn't matter where she was or which brother she was with, whenever they were close she became horny. She loved them so much and wanted to spend as much time loving them as she could, but that wasn't as often as she liked.

They were always on guard, and the only time they seemed to relax was when they were cuddled up with her at night. She was just thankful that the room they were staying in was at the opposite end of the house to the Heritage men.

Sabrina hugged him tight and smiled when he kissed the top of her head. She loved how tactile and affectionate her men were. They were all so tall, handsome, and muscular, and if it wasn't for the fact she was in danger, she would have wanted them to make a commitment with her, but she couldn't ask that of them. Not when things were so uncertain. She didn't understand why they meant so much to her so quickly, but they did and she wasn't about to question it. There was so much other stuff going on to worry about her feelings for Trick, Trent, and Tristan right now.

She sighed with contentment when Trent pressed against her back. She always felt so safe and secure when she was between them, and as much as she'd love to spend the rest of the night making love with them and cuddled up between them, she couldn't.

She drew back when she heard footsteps heading their way and was pleased when Trent kept an arm around her waist as the others entered the kitchen. She saw Damon and presumed the two men with him were his brothers. But what shocked her was seeing how happy the petite dark-haired woman was. She seemed to glow from the inside out, and when her eyes landed on her men, Sabrina could see how much she loved them and they loved her. What she wouldn't give to have a permanent relationship like that.

Trick nudged Trent aside and stood next to her. "Sabrina, this is Sam, Tyson, and their wife Rachel. Damon you've already met."

"Hi." Sabrina smiled. "It's nice to meet you all."

"Hi, Sabrina." Rachel moved forward and pulled her into a hug, surprising her. "I've heard so much about you. I feel like I already know you. I just know we are going to be great friends."

"Thank you," Sabrina replied in a husky voice at Rachel's friendly, open acceptance.

"Why don't we let the boys make the coffee or get the beer or whatever?" Rachel turned and quirked an eyebrow at her men. "We can go into the living room and talk."

Sab glanced at Trick, and when he gave her a slight nod, she replied, "Sure."

She and Rachel headed to the sofas, leaving the men in the kitchen.

"I'll bet you're pleased that Noble was spotted and arrested."

"What?" Sab leaned forward with a frown. "When did that happen?"

"Earlier this afternoon. I'm sure that Damon said he'd called Trick to let him know."

"He must have forgotten to tell me." Sabrina glared at the door to the kitchen but couldn't see anyone. She could hear the men talking quietly and wondered what was going on, but she was feeling a bit too angry about being left in the dark to talk to them right now. Plus, they had visitors and she didn't want to go storming in there to confront them about withholding information.

"Yeah, maybe," Sabrina finally remembered to reply. "So how long have you been in Slick Rock? Did you grow up here?"

"I've been here for three years now. I was actually on the run for six months and when I ran out of cash I needed to get a job."

"Damn. What happened to you?" Sabrina asked and reached out to clasp Rachel's hand in support when she saw her eyes cloud over.

"I witnessed a cop committing murder and he saw me. I actually worked for the police commissioner in Miami and ran to him and told him what happened. That asshole threatened me since the detective I'd seen commit the crime was related to him by marriage."

"Shit." Sabrina squeezed her hand in sympathy.

"I ended up applying for a job with the sheriff's department and met Damon, Sam, and Ty. Turned out to be the best thing that ever happened to me. Maybe things happen for a reason. I can see how much you love the Wendall men. I think you were supposed to end up here at this time so they could help protect you and fall in love with you."

"I hate putting everyone in danger. I don't think I could live with my conscience if anything happened to them or some other innocent person." Sabrina sighed and threaded her fingers through her hair.

"I knew we were going to be friends," Rachel said with a smile. "That's exactly the way I thought a few years back, but, honey, the

men in this town are tough. You need to trust them and know that
they will do everything in their power to keep you safe."

"I know." Sabrina sighed again.

"Now tell me all about this Noble guy and why he is out to get
you," Rachel said.

She and Rachel spent the next hour and a half talking. Trick,
Tristan, and Trent came in now and then to check up on them, and
every time Trick looked at her she glared at him to let him know she
was pissed at him. The men eventually converged in the living room,
and they all talked and laughed. The time sped by, and Sabrina didn't
even realize how late it was until their visitors got up to leave.

"Oh, Sab, come and check out my new truck," Rachel said and
tugged her down the verandah steps to the gleaming blue truck parked
close to the house.

"This is yours?" Sabrina asked. "I love this."

"Yeah, it's great. I love driving it even if I nearly need a
stepladder to get up into it."

Sabrina got into the front passenger seat after Rachel unlocked it
and she got into the driver's seat. She inhaled the new car smell and
looked at the dash. She had always wanted to drive a truck but had
never had enough cash for the one she wanted and, since she had
student loans to pay, she hadn't wanted to get a bank loan.

"How long have you had it?"

"Two weeks," Rachel replied as she ran her hand over the edge of
her leather seat. "I've always wanted one but could never afford it.
My men bought it for me for my birthday."

"Happy belated birthday," Sab said with a smile. "I love the
color."

"Yeah, it's great. Maybe when this is all over"—Rachel paused to
point toward the talking men on the porch—"we can go for a spin. I'll
even let you drive it."

"You will?"

"Of course. That's what friends do."

They turned to look at the men as they walked over to the truck. Tristan reached in, clasped her waist, and lifted her down before she could blink. "I look forward to it, Rachel."

"You bet, girlfriend. I can't wait for you to meet all the other women. Thanks for such a great night."

"It should be me thanking you. It was nice to talk to another woman for a change." Sabrina grinned when Rachel burst out laughing.

"Yeah, the testosterone can be a bit much at times."

"You said it."

"Hey." Tristan chuckled as he placed her on her feet. "I represent that remark."

"You certainly do," Sab replied. "As do your brothers."

"And every other man in this town," Rachel called out. "Take care, Sabrina."

"You, too, Rachel."

The men piled into the truck, and with a wave, Rachel turned the vehicle around and drove down the drive.

Sabrina sighed and leaned back against Tristan.

"Are you all right, darlin'?"

"Yeah. I had a good time, but I'm feeling a little tired."

Trick and Trent moved to stand in front of her, and when she remembered what Rachel told her about Harvey Noble being caught, her anger rose again. She pulled out of Tristan's arms and walked closer to Trick.

"Why didn't you tell me that Noble had been arrested?"

"Uh…" Trick glanced at his brothers before meeting her gaze again. "I didn't want you upset again. You've been having enough trouble sleeping as it is."

"You arrogant jerk," Sabrina snapped and poked him in the chest. "This isn't about you and what you think. I have every right to know what is going on. Don't you think that it would have put my mind at ease to know that that fucker had been captured? Damn you, Trick.

This isn't going to work if you keep important information to yourself."

"Sab, I'm sorry. I just thought that it would be better to stay quiet since you seemed a little less on edge. I didn't want to upset you."

"I'd rather be upset and aware than ignorant and vulnerable because you and your brothers haven't told me what's happening." She met Tristan's and then Trent's eyes. "Did you two know?"

They both slowly nodded their heads, and she started shaking with fury. "Would any of you have told me if Noble had been spotted in town? Or would you have left me in the dark so I wouldn't have to worry my pretty little head over it?"

Trick opened and closed his mouth, floundering for a response. Tristan and Trent looked at the ground, and she knew she had her answer. She was so angry she was getting hot and had no doubt her face was probably bright pink.

Sabrina knew these men were the take-charge kind, but she expected to be treated with respect and as an equal. Just because she didn't have their brawn didn't mean she was helpless. Right now she was hurt and confused. She loved them all so much, but she needed some space.

She turned and walked around Tristan and headed back to the house. She was glad the Heritage men were already inside and hoped they hadn't witnessed her ire. She paused on the top step and looked back at them over her shoulder.

"I think it would be better if you three spent the night in the other bedrooms tonight. I need some time to think." She entered the house and, once she was in the bedroom, quietly closed the door and moved toward the bathroom. She needed a shower, and then she was going to try and get some sleep.

She was so damn tired. Tired of living in fear. Tired of being told what to do and tired of not being able to live the way she wanted. But most of all she was hurt. Hurt that they hadn't thought she needed to be updated. Her heart was aching and she wanted to cry, but she wasn't going to. She had never been one to shed tears, and she wasn't about to do it now.

* * * *

Sawyer hid in the shadows of the large barn. His plan had paid off. Moving to the next town over and swapping rental cars had been the right thing to do. He made sure to work at night and stay concealed in the shadows. It had been easy to follow one of the sheriffs home one night, and after he'd driven down the block he'd parked his car and walked back.

He'd been lucky enough to see the sheriff's woman arrive home from somewhere, and after the sheriff helped her out of what looked to be a new truck, Sawyer had made his move. Sawyer had every gizmo imaginable. He remembered some of the other bodyguards teasing him and nicknaming him "gadget man," but he hadn't cared. He had everything he needed for a one-man military operation and didn't need help from anyone. It was easy to place a tracker on that truck. A woman wouldn't notice a tail, and he'd hoped that the sheriff's bitch would lead him to that slut without him ever having to sight her truck. His tracker had worked perfectly, and he'd arrived ten minutes later. It had been a long wait before he'd caught a glimpse of Noble's target, but his patience had paid off.

Sawyer wished he'd been close enough to hear what Sabrina had been ranting about, but he was too far away. He'd had to bite back his laughter when the cunt had started poking one of the guys in the chest and giving him what for, but he'd kept his mouth shut. When she'd stormed inside, he'd kept his eyes on the darkened windows, hoping she would go into one of them on this side of the house. If he knew what bedroom she was sleeping in, he would be able to slip inside and take her. She hadn't let him down. He'd been able to see into the bedroom before she'd lowered the blinds.

Maybe he could use her to get some cash out of Noble. He didn't really want to kill the bitch, but he would if he had to. She was a looker, and he would love to fuck her. As his cock stirred in his pants, he imagined holding her down as he took her. He bet she'd fight him. He loved it when women struggled. It turned him on big time.

Noble wouldn't care if he brought him damaged goods. Yeah, he was going to keep the bitch alive, and after slaking his lust with her he was going to use her for collateral. As far as he was concerned Noble owed him big-time. If it hadn't been for him, that chip would never have come to fruition. He wished he'd never told that asshole of his plans because that prick had stolen his idea right out from under his nose.

He'd been on a high after raping a woman, and he'd had a few beers. Before he knew it he'd been telling his boss about his idea of making a spyware chip. The only reason he hadn't killed Noble back then was because he'd sent one of his other minions to follow him and the prick had filmed him in action. Noble had threatened to send the evidence to the cops.

Sawyer had been biding his time because he knew in his heart that Noble would get what was coming to him. Noble was going to die by his hand, but first he needed to get his hands on all that cash, and now that he knew where that bitch was, he'd have a bargaining chip.

He had been going to make his move tonight but decided to wait a little longer. If they became complacent, it would make his job easier when it came time to take her. Plus, with six men living in that house and from seeing how feisty the bitch was, he didn't want to get caught.

He'd have to think of a way to distract all the men. He smiled and rubbed his hands together as he stayed to the shadows and walked back to where he'd hidden his rental car.

He couldn't wait to fuck that bitch, and when he'd satisfied his lust, he was going to fuck Noble over, too.

Chapter Eleven

Tristan glared at Trick as he sat on the edge of the single bed in the other guest room. Trent was lying on the other bed, looking relaxed with his hands behind his head, but from the way his brother's biceps were flexing and the muscle ticking in his jaw, he was anything but.

"What the fuck are we going to do now?" Trent asked as he pushed up from the bed and swung his legs over the side.

"We give her the time she needs to calm down," Trick said before scrubbing a hand over his face.

"She's pissed and she has every right to be." Tristan stated the obvious, but he was angry, too. He and his brothers should have been cuddled up with their woman in her bed, and if he hadn't let Trick talk him into keeping information from Sabrina, they would have been.

"I can't understand why she's so angry." Trick started to pace in between the beds. "I was only trying to protect her. She's been so uptight, and for once she was relaxed. I just wanted her to stay that way."

"She thinks we don't trust her."

"What?" Trick snapped. "Why the hell would she think that?"

"For an older brother, you can be really dumb where women are concerned," Trent snarled. "We kept vital information from her. Yes, it was with the best intentions, but she is an independent woman."

"It's not really about trust," Tristan said. "She's pissed because we were treating her like a child. Which she's not."

"I know that." Trick sighed and then stopped to stare out the window.

Tristan hated that they were close to her but so far away. She was two doors down because the bedroom between them had been made into an office. He wanted to be in the room beside hers if they couldn't be in her room, but that wasn't an option. At least not tonight.

"Let's just give her the space she needs tonight and hopefully after a good night's sleep she'll be more receptive to listening," Tristan said. "You are going to have to apologize and explain to her why you kept Noble's arrest from her. And we'll apologize, too." He met Trent's eyes, and his brother nodded.

"Where are you going to sleep?" Trent asked Trick since he and Tristan had already taken dibs on the two single beds.

"The couch." Trick turned away from the window and headed for the door but stopped when Tristan started talking.

"We make her breakfast in bed and then say we're sorry."

"Agreed," Trick replied before he disappeared out to the living room.

Tristan shucked his jeans and socks but kept his T-shirt on. It was a cool night, and since the single beds were too small for his large frame, he was going to need all the warmth he could get. The Heritage men had set this room up for when their nieces came to stay, and even though he would be sleeping on pink sheets and under a princess quilt cover, he was just thankful he had somewhere to lay his head for the night. Tomorrow they would do everything they could to right their wrong with Sabrina.

* * * *

Sabrina's nose twitched when something tickled it. She rubbed it with her fingers and started drifting back down to a deeper sleep, but something tickled her nose again. This time she swatted her hand out, trying to knock what she thought was a pesky fly away, but her hand connected with flesh. She gasped as her eyes snapped open and blinked when she saw Trick's shocked expression with his hand against his cheek.

She was horrified when she realized she'd slapped him in the face and quickly pushed up until she was sitting against the headboard with a pillow shoved behind her back. "Oh my god. I'm so sorry."

A chuckle near the foot of the bed drew her attention, and she spotted Tristan and Trent standing there watching her.

"That's some great reflexes you have, baby." Trent grinned and then moved around the bed to place the breakfast tray on the bedside table.

The aroma of coffee, bacon, and eggs permeated the air, and saliva filled her mouth and her stomach started growling. Although she wanted to reach for the tray and dive right in to appease her empty belly, she was worried she had hurt Trick. He was still sitting on the edge of the bed with his hand against his cheek and a stunned look on his face.

"Are you okay? Did I hurt you?"

Trick lowered his hand, and she felt guilty and embarrassed to see his cheek was a little pink. Thank God she hadn't put all her force behind it, otherwise he would be sporting her handprint on his skin.

"I'm fine. Consider that payback for yesterday," he said in a quiet voice.

"Payback?" she asked. "What do you mean?"

Trick drew in a deep breath before exhaling on a sigh. "I am really sorry for not telling you about Luke's phone call. I should have told you straight away and I should never have ordered my brothers to keep a secret from you either."

Sabrina studied him and could see that he meant every contrite word he'd spoken, but she wanted to know why he hadn't told her. "Why didn't you?"

"It wasn't because I don't trust you or didn't think you couldn't handle the information or was treating you like a child. It was...I..." He reached out and took her hand in his. "You were a little more relaxed than you'd been since we'd met you and I didn't want to make you tense again. You were smiling more and I love seeing you that way. You seemed so happy. Although my reasons for not telling you were meant to protect you, I should have informed you right away."

"Yes, you should have. I know that just because Noble has been arrested doesn't mean I'm safe, and yes, I enjoyed getting out in the sunshine and was feeling better, but I just need to know what's going on. This is all because of me, and of course I've been tense and scared, but I'm stronger than you seem to think I am, Trick. I appreciate that you were looking out for me though."

"I love you, honey. Please forgive me?"

"I do." Sabrina brought his hand to her mouth and kissed his knuckles. "I love you, too." She looked at Tristan and Trent. "I love all of you, but you can't keep me in the dark."

"We won't." Tristan sat on the other side of the bed and placed his hand on her thigh over the quilt. "I love you, too, darlin'."

Tristan reached for the breakfast tray and put it on her lap. "We brought you breakfast as a peace offering. I love you so much, Sab. I don't ever want to spend another night away from you. I missed snuggling up next to you and holding you."

"I missed that, too. Just all of you promise to tell me as soon as more information comes to light."

"We promise," Trick said before he leaned over and placed a light kiss on her lips.

Trent picked up her coffee mug and handed it to her. She took a few sips before eating breakfast.

"What's happening today?" she asked when she was finished.

"Tristan and I are going to help do the chores. Trent is going to spend the day with you."

"Did you have anything planned today, baby?" Trent asked.

"Well, since Hank, David, and Barry have been putting up with us I thought I'd do some baking for them."

"You like baking?" Trent's face lit up, and he rubbed his hands together.

"Yeah, I love to cook."

"You're a fantastic cook, honey," Trick said.

"Thanks."

"Hank and his brothers said they want to keep you around because they've never eaten so well," Tristan said with a mock scowl.

"Come on, Tristan," Trick said before kissing her on the forehead and getting to his feet. "We'd better get out there. We have downed fences to fix."

"Okay." Tristan stood up shoved Trick out of the way and then kissed her lips. "Have a good day, darlin'."

"You, too."

Trent took the tray from her lap. "Go and shower, baby. I'll have another cup of coffee ready for when you come out."

Sabrina watched his delectable ass until he was gone. She was glad they'd cleared the air. She'd had trouble sleeping last night and had berated herself for acting so harsh with them. She'd gotten used to having them sleep with her and had missed them a lot, but for a relationship to work between three men and one woman, she had to set some boundaries. And trying to make decisions for her and keeping pertinent information to themselves wasn't one as far as she was concerned. She felt lighthearted and happy after taking a stand and the air had been cleared, and just hoped that they would want to take the next step in their relationship when it was safe to like she wanted to.

She had an urge deep down inside to have their babies. The Wendall men were sweet, loving, and protective. She could see herself spending the rest of her life with them.

After she'd showered and dressed, she headed to the kitchen. Trent had the dishwasher going and was pouring coffee into mugs.

She sat down next to him at the table.

"What are you going to make, baby?"

"Apple pie, chocolate cake, and maybe some cookies."

"I love apple pie. If there are enough ingredients and you feel up to it, you'd better make two or maybe three. I know damn well that if you bake as good as you cook there won't be any pie left by the end of the night."

"Yeah, okay. The way you all eat, I can see I had better make at least four if there are enough ingredients."

Trent flexed his arm, making his bicep bulge. "We're growing boys."

Sabrina laughed when he chuckled.

"You never mention your parents, baby. Why is that?" Trent must have seen something in her face, because the next thing she knew, he was picking her up and plonking her into his lap.

"I don't have any."

"What happened to them, Sab?"

"I have no idea. All I was ever told was that I was found in a basket on the steps of the orphanage when I was around a week old. There were never any papers or a note with what little I had. Apparently the authorities put out bulletins on the local news and radio stations asking for anyone who had witnessed me being dumped to come forward, but no one ever did."

"I'm sorry, baby. That must have been hard."

"No," Sabrina sighed. "The hardest thing was when all the other kids got adopted but no one ever seemed to want me." She swallowed around the lump in her throat as the emotion of rejection swamped her, but she had vowed at the age of fifteen she was never going to shed another tear over parents she'd never known, ever again. And she wouldn't be crying over strangers who didn't want to adopt her either.

From that moment on, she'd concentrated on her studies with every intention of going to college and getting her degree so she would have a good life. Funny how that all seemed so unimportant when you had a target on your back. Being in danger made her realize what was important. Material things and money weren't necessary in the scheme of things. Although, having cash did make life easier, but what was important to her was love. And now that she had it, she wasn't going to let anything or anyone stand in her way.

An epiphany hit her upside the head. There was no way in hell she was leaving to live her life on the run. She didn't want her men, or anyone else for that matter, getting hurt because of her, but they had to be able to make their own choices just like she did. It would kill her if they ended up injured, but running in the hope they would be safe was cowardly. It took strength to stay and make a stand. If they were in danger, she needed to be here so she could help to protect her men, too. Even if she had to throw herself in front of a bullet to do so.

Trent hugged her tight and rested his head on top of hers, before rubbing his cheek against her own. "We want you, baby. Don't ever doubt that. You mean everything to me and my brothers."

Sabrina shifted until she was straddling him and wrapped her arms around his neck. "I love you, too, Trent." How long they stayed like that, she had no idea and didn't really care. She loved being in his, Tristan's, or Trick's arms. Her heart was filled with joy. She had found men worthy of living her life with and who found her worthy, too. She wasn't about to jeopardize what they had by taking off. It would break her heart, and she was sure theirs, too. She couldn't do that to them, and she didn't want to do that to herself either.

She intended to hold on with both hands.

Sabrina finally released Trent, and they got to work baking. By the time they started on making sandwiches for lunch, there were four apple pies cooling on the counter, a frosted chocolate cake in the fridge, and a jar's worth of Anzac cookies that had extra golden syrup in them.

She caught Trent snatching two cookies off the cooling rack, and before she could tell him off, he shoved both cookies into his mouth at once. She laughed so hard when she'd seen his bulging cheeks and the way he was having trouble trying to chew with his too-full mouth, and he ended up laughing, too. He sprayed crumbs everywhere and then had started to choke when he inhaled. It was difficult to thump him on the back when she was laughing so hard she was crying and having trouble breathing herself.

"Serves you right." Sabrina chuckled as she wiped the tears from her face. "You shouldn't have put so much in your mouth."

When Trent swallowed what was in his mouth and got his breath back, he gave her a forlorn puppy dog look. "I thought you'd get mad at me for stealing the cookies and didn't want you taking them back."

"No. I was going to give you some on a plate and make you some coffee to go with them, but since you couldn't wait, too late."

"Aw, come on, Sab. I love dunking cookies in coffee," he said as he pulled her into his arms and hugged her.

"Nope. You're going to have to wait until after dinner tonight."

"You are a hard woman, Sabrina Brown." Trent winked at her to let her know he was teasing.

She withdrew from his arms, grabbed the cloth, threw it at him, and pointed at the cookie crumbs. "You'd better clean up your mess so we can start on making sandwiches for lunch. The others are going to be here soon."

"Taskmaster," Trent muttered under his breath but turned to clean up his mess. When he turned his back on her, she pinched him on the ass. He looked at her back over his shoulder. "Promise?"

Sabrina laughed, shook her head, and went to get the ingredients from the fridge for the sandwiches.

Just as she and Trent put everything on the table, the men came in.

"Something smells good enough to eat," Hank said as he sniffed loudly. His eyes zeroed in on the four pies cooling.

"Is that apple pie I smell?" Barry asked as he sauntered in behind Hank.

"I smell cookies." David inhaled deeply.

"Yes. Trent and I made apple pies, chocolate chip and Anzac cookies, and chocolate cake, but none of you get any until you've had lunch. The pies are for dessert tonight."

Hank shifted direction and headed over to her. The next thing she knew she was swept from her feet and being spun in a circle. She shrieked and clutched at his shoulders.

"Get your hands off our woman," Trick yelled, and for a moment she thought he was angry, until she saw he was smiling.

Hank placed her back on her feet and hugged her. "Nope, don't think I will. I think my brothers and I are going to keep her."

"Not going to happen." Trent moved in behind her and pulled her away from Hank and into his arms.

"Get your own damn woman," Tristan said and then winked at her when she glanced at him.

"Okay, fun's over," Sabrina said and pointed to the table. "Sit. Eat."

"Yes, ma'am." Hank kissed her on the forehead before doing as she'd told him to.

"Thanks, Sabby." David kissed her cheek and sat down.

"If these guys ever piss you off, you come to us, sweetie. There will always be a bed in this house for you," David said with a stoic expression on his face, but the gleam in his eye belied his tone.

Once the men had eaten their fill and devoured the chocolate cake, the men went back to work. Sabrina and Trent cleaned up, and after starting a beef-and-vegetable stew, he guided her to the living room and they snuggled on the sofa.

It felt so nice being in his arms, and since he was spooning her from behind, his breath was wafting over the skin of her neck and ear. Just those little puffs of breath were enough to make her desire for him kick in. Her areolae began to contract, and her nipples peaked. Her pussy started to moisten, and her clit began to throb.

She wanted to turn over and ravish him but didn't want to break their contented mood, so she stayed still. But when she felt the bulge against her ass and lower back growing, she decided there was no more perfect time to love him.

They had the whole house to themselves.

Chapter Twelve

Trent hadn't realized he could be so lighthearted until Sabrina had come into their lives. He'd enjoyed playing around with her while he'd helped her bake. He didn't really have a clue what he was doing, but he been directed by her guidance and loved every minute being with her.

Most of all, he relished having her in his arms. Her natural womanly scent, the aroma of her bodywash and her warm skin, was amazing. She shifted in his arms, and although he tried to stop his twitching cock from growing, it was a losing battle. When she moved again and the muscles in her thighs and ass tensed, he realized she was just as turned on as he was.

"Do you want me, baby?" he whispered against her ear and felt her shiver.

"Yes."

"Sit up, Sab." As much as he would like to make love to her where they were, it wasn't their house and he didn't want anyone other than him and his brothers seeing her naked. She sat up, and he scooted out from behind her and got to his feet, then held a hand out to her, and immediately she placed hers in his.

He helped her up from the sofa and led her toward the bedroom and closed the door.

"Take your clothes off, baby," he ordered as he started removing his own.

When they were both naked, he scooped her up and placed her in the middle of the bed before following her down. He didn't immediately pounce on her, but slowly and lightly caressed up and down her body, following the contours of her sexy curves and soft skin.

"I love how soft you feel under my hands," he said before leaning down and kissing her.

He moaned into her mouth when her hands began moving over him, too. He loved the way she touched, caressed, and fondled him and would never get tired of it. When he was in danger of coming in her hand as it slid up and down his shaft, he pulled it away and drew his lips away from hers. He needed her in the worst way. His cock was leaking pre-cum and bobbing with the beat of his heart.

"I want you to roll over onto your stomach, Sab. Will you do that for me?"

She gave him a puzzled frown but nodded and rolled over. He reached into the bedside table for the lube before caressing up and down her back and kneading her ass cheeks.

"Do you trust me, Sab?"

"Yes," she immediately replied.

"I want to fuck your ass, baby. Will you let me?"

"Oh God." She moaned as he spread her cheeks and pressed a finger against her anus. When she tried to press back against his finger he pulled it away, opened the tube, and squirted some onto his fingertip.

"Has anyone ever touched or fucked you here before?" He smoothed the gel around her asshole and pressed the tip of his finger into her.

"Not fucked. Only you and your brothers have touched me there," she groaned out as she lifted her hips from the bed.

"I'll be gentle with you, baby." Trent hooked his other arm around her hips and lifted her to her hands and knees. "Place your shoulders on the bed, Sab. That position will open you up more."

"Oh," she whispered as he pressed his finger into her further. "That feels so good. I never would have..." Her words trailed away as he begun to thrust his finger in and out of her star.

After a few strokes he added more lube to his fingers and then pressed in two. She wiggled, moaned, and counterthrust against him.

"More. Trent, I need you."

"Soon, Sabby," he rasped. What he wanted to do was shove his hard, aching cock deep into her ass, but she needed to be stretched out so he wouldn't hurt her, and her comfort and pleasure was important to him, so he took his time preparing her. When he had her stretched out, he rolled a condom onto his cock, slathered it in personal gel, and moved up behind her. Just as he pressed the tip of his dick to her anus, the door to the bedroom opened. He glanced over his shoulder to see Tristan enter before quietly closing the door behind him. His brother's eyes zeroed in on Sabrina, and he started to quickly shuck his clothes.

* * * *

Sabrina had no idea that her ass was so sensitive, but now that she'd had Trent's fingers in there, she wanted more. When she felt the tip of his cock against her rosette, she took a deep breath and tried to relax. She knew it was going to hurt a little having a large, hard dick in her ass for the first time, but she needed him to fill her so bad.

He pushed against her, and she moaned when the head popped through her tight muscle. Although it felt strange and there was a slight burning sensation, it felt so damn good.

"You okay, baby?" Trent asked around panting breaths.

"Yes. Give it to me, Trent. Please?" She pressed back against him, but he gripped her hips to hold her still. She growled with frustration and was about to open her eyes to look back at him over her shoulder when she felt the mattress dip beside her. Her lids popped open, and then she was looking into Tristan's hungry eyes.

He didn't give her time to ask when he'd gotten there, because he leaned over and started kissing her rapaciously. She whimpered into his mouth as Trent pressed into her a little further, and then she moaned when he pinched one nipple between his finger and thumb, before doing the same to the other.

Tristan broke the kiss and scooted back slightly. "Get up on your hands, darlin'."

Sabrina pushed up to her hands and moaned when Trent stroked into her more.

"Fuck! You feel amazing, Sab. So hot and tight."

He was the one who felt amazing, but she was so full, horny, and breathless she couldn't have spoken right then to tell him so.

She looked at Tristan when he clasped her upper arms and then helped her into an upright position on her knees. He rolled and slid his legs between her spread ones until he was lying on his back beneath her, and then he pulled her back down to his chest.

"We're going to love you together, Sab. Are you ready?" Tristan asked.

She gulped, feeling a little nervous since she'd never had two men inside her at once before, but wanting it so bad her pussy clenched and dripped.

Trent moaned, and his fingers clutched her hips tighter. "Hurry the fuck up, Tris. I'm not gonna last long."

Tristan wiggled his hips until she felt his condom-covered cock at her entrance, and then he shoved up into her in one gentle, searing thrust.

"Oh. Oh. Oh."

Tristan froze and gripped her hair, turning her gaze to his. "Did I hurt you, Sab?"

"No." She clenched around him. "Need…more."

"Let's give our woman what she needs," Trent said in a voice hoarse with desire before he slowly withdrew his cock from her ass to the tip.

As he pumped back in, Tristan withdrew and she found herself rising in a maelstrom of passion so intense she was shaking.

With each stroke of their cocks in and out of her ass and cunt, they increased the intensity of their thrusts until the only sounds in the room were their moans, groans, heavy breathing, and the slapping of their connecting bodies.

The heat from the friction built slowly, and the ache inside her grew more intense. Cream dripped from her pussy, but she didn't care. All the mattered was the two men loving her and building the nirvanic pleasure inside her.

"I. Can't. Hold. Off." Trent moaned as he slammed his pelvis against her ass, sending another riot of nerve endings zinging sparks of pleasure throughout her body. "Help her out."

Sabrina gasped and moaned when Trent shifted her up until she was sitting upright, and then Tristan started rubbing her clit with the tip of his finger. He wasn't gentle, but he didn't hurt her. He pressed firmly and rubbed fast.

That was all it took to send her up and over the edge. Her eyelids slammed closed, her head tilted back, and she screamed softly. Her internal muscles grabbed and let go, clenched and released the cocks in her ass and pussy. Cream gushed from her cunt, and a white light streaked before her eyes. All the time she was coming, Trent and Tristan continued to stroke their big, hard dicks in and out of her holes.

Just as the most explosive orgasm she'd ever had began to wane, Tristan pinched her clit and sent her back up into the stratosphere. Her whole body quaked and quivered, more cream spurted from her pussy, and she thought she was about to pass out.

She only vaguely heard first Trent and then Tristan shout as they drove into her as they, too, reached their peaks. By the time she once more became aware of her surroundings, she was lying on the mattress in between them and they were caressing her body.

"You okay, Sabby?" Tristan asked.

"Amazing."

"We didn't hurt you, did we?" Trent asked.

"No. That was…You guys blew my mind."

Tristan chuckled and kissed her lovingly on the lips. "That was the whole idea, darlin'." He rolled from the bed and started to get dressed. "I'd better get back out there before Trick comes looking for me. I'll see you at dinner, Sab."

Sabrina nodded and, when he was gone, rolled over and cuddled up to Trent. He wrapped his arms around her and held her close.

"Would you want to do that again, baby?"

"Hell yes," she answered emphatically, which drew a chuckle from him.

"I knew you were the perfect woman for us."

"I'm not perfect, Trent."

"To us you are."

"You make me feel so special."

Trent shifted until she could see his face. "You are special, Sabrina. You're everything."

"You say the sweetest things." She reached up and kissed him. "No one is perfect, but if you can overlook my faults then I guess I can overlook them, too."

"You don't have any," Trent said with a gleam in his eye.

"Of course I do."

"Like what?"

"I hate being told what to do."

"No?" Trent asked in a playful tone.

"If I get pissed off, I yell."

"Like you did last night?"

"Worse."

"Baby, we all get mad. I'm impatient most of the time and I can get real bossy, although I don't think I'm as bossy as Trick. Tristan is just as bad as I am. None of us are flawless, but as long as we keep the lines of communication open, we'll be fine."

Sabrina knew he was right. Communication was the biggest part of keeping a relationship healthy.

* * * *

Sawyer couldn't wait any longer. He had a bad feeling in his gut, and he feared that Noble had been caught. He'd tried contacting the asshole on his burner phone, but the prick either had it turned off or was just ignoring him, because it went straight to voice mail. He was beginning to think he would never get his hands on that money, but he wasn't about to give up now. He was so close to his goal, and he wasn't about to let anyone or anything get in the way of him getting that cash. Even if Noble had been arrested by the authorities, the assholes may not have found his rental or the dump of a motel he'd been holed up in, and he wouldn't have any trouble breaking into that car.

Yes, it's definitely time to put my plan in to action.

He waited until the lights in the house were turned off and then crept toward the barn. He sat in the shadows for another hour, and then he picked up the two gas cans he'd had to lug from his own rental. It had been easy to buy the gas cans at the hardware store a couple of hours away, and no one had questioned him when he filled them up.

He worked quickly, splashing the flammable liquid around the outside of the timber building, and when the cans were empty, he carried them over close to the house and stashed them behind a large shrub after making sure he'd wiped them down so his prints wouldn't be found.

After making sure no one was about, he scurried back to the side of the barn, pulled the matches from his pocket, lit one, and flicked it. The fire was instantaneous, and he jogged quietly back to the house and around to the window where he'd seen that bitch go the previous night.

Now all he had to do was watch and wait for the perfect opportunity and that cunt would be his.

It wasn't long before the horses inside the barn started neighing shrilly and loudly. It took all of five minutes after that for the men to start running from the house. First there were only three of them, but he knew there was a total of six men inside. He hunkered down lower and remained still. Two more of the men came out and started on trying to douse the flames.

Sawyer hoped the last asshole emerged soon, or he was going to have to take him out. He didn't want to end up in a fight because that bitch might just get away from him before he could snatch her.

He nearly sighed with relief when the other man came running out yelling at the top of his voice that the fire department were on their way.

He had to move and he had to move now, otherwise he might get caught kidnapping the bitch. After looking at the men intently and seeing they had all the horses out from the barn and were working on the fire, he made his move.

Still staying as close to the side of the house as possible and in the shadows, he headed for the open back door. They had made this much easier than he thought. She was in the house alone, and after one last glance at the men, he hurried up the porch steps and into the house.

He smiled when he found her in the kitchen talking on the phone with her back to him. She didn't even know he was there. Sawyer had learned a long time ago to be stealthy. One of his buddies had been in the military, and he had shown him all the tricks of the trade. He knew how to move without having his clothes brush against his body and how to walk without making a sound.

She'd just said good-bye to whomever she was talking to and hung up the phone. Her body tensed as if she were about to turn around.

He made his move. One of his large hands covered her mouth and nose, and his other wrapped around her arms and chest from behind. Her scream was muffled, but the bitch had gumption and fought against him. One of her legs kicked back, her bare heel slamming into his shin, but he didn't release her.

All of a sudden she relaxed her body and let her legs buckle, but he was ready for any move she tried to make and tightened his arm around her chest, squeezing hard. He lifted her up against him and stumbled when she planted her feet against the edge of the counter and pushed off hard.

But he could feel her weakening. Without any air getting into her lungs it wouldn't take long before she passed out, which would make getting her off the property much easier for him. She tried pulling her arms up out of his hold, but she was fading fast, and then she slumped in his hold.

He kept his hand over her nose and mouth a bit longer until he was certain she wasn't shitting him, and then he withdrew it, clasped her waist, turned her around, and slung her over his shoulder.

He was out the front door moments later. When the fire trucks came roaring up the drive, he hid behind the trees lining it and then continued on to his car, which he'd parked behind a large bush past the entrance to the ranch.

After opening the trunk, he slung the bitch into it, taped her wrists and ankles together, and taped a piece over her mouth. He didn't want her making any noise in case he was stopped by the cops or when he went to Noble's motel room.

If Noble was incarcerated and the police or agents had found his hideout, he wasn't about the let her give him away.

Chapter Thirteen

Sabrina came awake with a start, and fear made her tremble when she remembered the man coming up behind her suffocating her with his hand. She could hear the drone of tires on asphalt and tried to use her hands to push up. The fear nearly overwhelmed her when she realized her wrists and ankles were tied together. The only consolation was that even though her mouth was covered with what felt like tape, she could still breathe through her nose.

She looked around and took in the dark trunk she was in, but there was a little light coming from the tail and brake lights when they were applied. She wanted to give in to the fear, close her eyes, and go to sleep, but that wasn't the way she worked. After taking a few deep breaths through her nose, her heart rate began to slow and the trembling in her body waned slightly. She had to keep it together so she could figure a way to get out of here, and if that wasn't possible she would need all her strength to fight.

Even though she had no idea who had abducted her, she knew it was Noble or one of his asshole thugs. She'd caught a glimpse of a big, muscular, bald man watching the office building as she left after she'd finished work, and even though she'd quickly glanced away, she'd felt him continue watching her until she'd turned a corner. Now that she thought back, she was sure she'd seen him more than once. The bastard had given her the creeps then, and if he was the one who had kidnapped her, she knew she was in serious trouble.

If her mouth hadn't been covered, her laughter would have been loud and hysterical. She was in trouble no matter who had her.

She just hoped she lived to see her men again.

* * * *

"All the horses are safe in the far corral," Trick yelled and rushed forward with a large, wet burlap bag. Hank had a fire hose directed at the worst of the flames while Barry, David, Trent, and Tristan were trying to beat the flames out the same as he was.

The fire trucks arrived just as the fire on the side of barn started to take hold. They stepped back as soon as the hoses began spraying water onto the flames.

"This fire had to be deliberately lit," Hank snarled angrily as he looked around.

"I have to agree," Trick replied. "The fire didn't start inside. If I had to hazard a guess I say some sort of accelerant was splashed around before being lit."

"Why would...Fuck! Sabrina!" Trent roared and took off running.

Trick's heart skipped a beat before racing painfully in his chest, and he took off after his brother. Tristan was on his heels.

Trent went racing toward one end of the house and Trick the other. The both came back out at the same time and entered the kitchen to find Tristan staring at the house phone handset dangling on its cord.

Trick spun around, flicking lights on as he headed toward the front door while dialing Luke on his cell.

"What's up?" Luke asked.

"Sabrina's missing. We fucked up, Luke. A fire was started at the barn as a distraction and the asshole took her while we were trying to save the horses and put the fire out."

"I'm on my way. Don't touch anything and make sure you don't trample over or tamper with any evidence."

"Trick!" Tristan yelled. "I found a set of footprints. It looks like he was carrying something heavy."

"Sabrina."

"Shit. What did that asshole do to her?" Trent asked angrily. "Tris, go get a flashlight and let's see if we can follow his trail."

Tristan took off to do as bid. Trick tried to follow the prints, but it got too hard the further away from the house he moved. He stopped and waited for his brother to come back with the portable light so he could continue on without messing up the tracks.

Tristan came back with a couple of flashlights. Trick, Trent, and Tristan followed the footprints until they came to the road. It took some more searching before they found impressions of tire treads in the gravel on the side of the road since they were nearly two hundred yards past the entrance to the Triple H Ranch. Just as they spotted them, flashing red-and-blue lights in the distance drew Trick's attention.

He waved the light so Luke would spot him and had never been more relieved to see his lawman friend. Luke stopped his car in the middle of the road, and he and Damon got out.

"What have you got?" Damon asked as he and Luke drew closer.

"Tire tracks," Tristan said and then explained how they had found footprints and followed them.

Luke scrubbed and hand over his face and sighed. "There is no way in hell we can track this fucker. We'd have to know what make, model of car he was driving and know what the license plate was."

"Damn it!" Trick snapped. "We can't just do nothing. Our woman is missing and in danger."

"Let's go back to the house," Luke said. "I'm going to contact the agent that has Noble. Maybe he's made the prick break and spill his guts, and if not then I have a contact who will do it."

Trick nodded, and they all headed to Luke's car and got in. None of them said a word as Luke drove them back to the ranch house. He and his brothers were lost in thought. He didn't need to speak to know that they were all very scared about what was happening to Sabrina.

* * * *

Sabrina had spent a long time trying to pry the covers off the tail and brake lights from inside the trunk. She had hoped that she could somehow send and SOS message and alert any other cars driving behind the one she was trapped in, but she hadn't been able to get the globes out. It was really difficult to maneuver with the limited amount of space she had and with her wrists tethered together. She'd broken all of her fingernails as she slipped them under the covers, trying to pull them off, not that she cared about that, but it pissed her off that she failed each and every time.

She was tired, cold, and scared. All she had on was a mid-thigh-length sleeping shirt and a pair of panties. At least she'd had that much. When she slept between her men she was usually naked, but it had been a chilly night and after making love with them and cleaning up she'd pulled her sleep shirt on. Thank God. She just wished she'd grabbed her robe before calling the fire department. She hadn't known that one of the men had already called from their cell phones. Maybe she should have called the sheriff's department instead. Not that it would have done her any good. She still had a feeling she'd be in the same predicament no matter who she called.

Now that she thought about it, she realized that the fire had been a diversion, and she wondered if her men even knew she was missing. Surely the fire department had arrived by now to fight the fire. It felt like hours had passed since she'd woken up in the trunk of the car.

What scared her most was not knowing who had her, where they were taking her, and what they wanted with her. If it was Harvey Noble, then she was living on borrowed time. She could still hear him telling that person on the phone to find her and kill her.

* * * *

Tristan was so pissed off with himself and his brothers because they'd been so easy to distract and now Sabrina was missing. He'd never felt so much fear in his life. He wanted to find whoever took her and tear him apart with his bare hands. He was barely keeping it together, and from the looks on his brother's faces, they weren't much better.

He felt so guilty for leaving her. He should have just stayed with her to protect her instead of rushing out to help get the horses out of the barn when Trick had called him. His older brother would have been mad, but Sabrina might have still been with them.

"I know what you're thinking," Luke said as he sat down at the table. "If one of you had stayed inside with Sabrina, you'd probably be dead."

"Shut up!" Tristan yelled and began pacing before turning back to face Luke. "At least I could have tried to save her."

"Could you have?" Damon asked. "What would you have done if he'd held a gun to her head? Would you have rushed him and taken a bullet? He would have killed you and still taken Sabrina."

Tristan knew he was right, but it still didn't take away his guilt.

"Stop torturing yourself on what you could have done differently and just concentrate on how we're going to save your woman," Luke said.

Just as Tristan was about to speak, Luke's cell rang. The sheriff answered and listened, making appropriate noises in response to the person on the other end before saying thanks and disconnecting the call.

"My friend in the FBI was able to get Noble to break. Noble has been hiding out in his hometown of Fort Collins in one of the rundown motels there. My friend called the local cops in, and after searching his room, they found a burner cell phone. The last few texts to Noble's phone were from someone called Sawyer. Not sure if that is his first or last name, but we and the feds are looking into it."

"Did they find out where this Sawyer is?" Trick asked.

"Yeah. He's been staying in Telluride about an hour and a half away, east of here."

Tristan started to feel hopeful that they would be able to find Sabrina now that they had a lead. "How many motels are in Telluride?" he asked.

"Many, but we got the name of the motel from Noble's burner phone. Apparently Sawyer's well and truly under his thumb and has been making daily reports by leaving voice messages and texts," Luke answered and then nodded at Damon.

Damon got up and moved across to the kitchen, pulling his cell phone from his pocket and then tapping on the screen. A moment later he was talking to someone.

"Damon is contacting the Telluride sheriff. He'll get him and his deputies to stake out that motel," Luke explained. "How long a lead do you think this Sawyer has?"

Trick glanced at his watch. "Can't be more than half an hour."

"Then let's move out," Luke said and stood up. His cell dinged to let him know he had a message. He pulled it up and then read the message before turning his phone around so Tristan and his brothers could see the screen and the photo of a bald man. "This is Jack Sawyer. He has a very nasty rap sheet. We need to go. Right now!"

* * * *

Sabrina cringed when the car went over a big bump or landed in a deep pothole in the road, jostling her body. Her head hit the floor of the trunk, and her hip felt like it was bruised after the hard jolt.

She started panting when the car slowed down and turned, and then went up over another big bump. That couldn't be good. She thought that the car had just driven over a speed bump, and the only time they were present was in a residential area or school zone. Her heart began to thump rapidly inside her chest, and her skin became clammy when she started to sweat. When the car stopped, she began shaking.

The engine turned off, and the door slammed as it was closed. She tensed her body, hoping to take her kidnapper unaware if he opened the trunk, but she also kept her eyes closed and tried to even her breathing out. She was ready. Ready for the fight of her life. She didn't know if she had a chance of getting away, but she wasn't about to go willingly. She wished she could have escaped him before he abducted her, but since that hadn't happened, she would do everything she needed to in order to get away from him, even if it meant taking his life or ending up dead herself.

It felt like a long time had passed before the trunk to the car was opened, and she opened her eyes slightly, watching from beneath lowered lashes. It felt like the blood drained from her face when she saw the bald guy from Fort Collins, and her skin began to crawl.

She took a quiet but deep breath, and when he reached in for her, she put every ounce of power into her legs and kicked out. Pride filled her when he grunted, but the guy must have the constitution of a rhinoceros, because his nose was bleeding but he didn't pull back. His fingers dug into the muscle in her thigh. Her squeal of pain was muffled by the tape over her mouth.

He dug harder until she could feel a bruise forming, and leaned over. "You try that again and I'll knock you out, but this time it won't be from lack of oxygen. Do you understand?" he asked angrily.

Sabrina nodded and tried to breathe through the pain. She whimpered with relief when he released her, and then he glanced around quickly before grabbing a hank of her hair and yanking her up and out of the trunk. She reached out to grip one of his arms with her hand, but he jerked her head back before she could touch him.

"Don't you fucking try anything, bitch. Just do as you're told and we'll get along fine."

He released her hair and slung her up over his shoulder and started walking. She tilted her head, trying to see where she was and where they were going through her hair. There was a building to the right, and he was moving toward it. She tossed her head and saw it was a motel. That meant people. People meant help.

Hope began to replace the fear. She was going to escape or get the attention of someone else, come hell or high water.

* * * *

Trent was glad to be riding with the sheriff. Even though Luke hadn't put his siren on, the red-and-blue lights were flashing as they sped through the night. He was thankful that Luke had been able to contact his FBI friend and get the information on where the fucker who had taken Sabrina was.

He'd been on the verge of tears when he realized she'd been taken, and he'd never been so scared in his life. He didn't know if he'd be able to continue living if she ended up dying because he and his brothers hadn't protected her. She was the love of his life, and he didn't want to go on without her by his side.

When they were ten minutes out of Telluride, the radio in Luke's car went off. "This is Sheriff Snow from Telluride. Sawyer has the woman and has just entered a motel room. We have all exits covered. She was conscious, but her arms and legs are bound. Do you want us to go in?"

"How many men do you have?" Damon asked.

"Just myself and my deputy."

"We'll be there in ten or less. Wait until we get there. This guy will be armed and is very dangerous."

"Copy that. Out."

Trent sat forward, feeling antsy now that they were closer to Sabrina. He wanted to be able to hold her in his arms again and tell her how much he loved her. When they saved her he was going to ask her to marry him. He didn't care if Trick and Tristan were ready to pop the question or not. He was going to take the initiative and wasn't going to take no for an answer.

* * * *

Sabrina watched the asshole from her seat near the window. He was sitting on the bed and tapping away at his laptop. Whatever he was seeing or doing wasn't making him happy. The more he read, the angrier he looked. She glanced about the room, looking for a weapon, but other than the bedside lamp, which was too far away, and the chair she was sitting on, she couldn't see anything else. Maybe if she could get him to let her go to the bathroom she would be able to find something in there. Anything was worth a try. She stomped her foot on the floor to get his attention, then pointed to the bathroom and the tape on her mouth. He put the laptop aside, walked over to her, plucked at the edge of the tape on her mouth, and stared coldly into her eyes as he ripped it off.

Sabrina sucked in a breath when it felt like a layer of her skin had been peeled away from her lips and around her mouth. She glared at the prick and tried to breathe through the burning pain. When she was able to, she said, "I need the bathroom."

He stepped back and moved aside before nodding his head.

"Can you get this tape off? It would make things a little easier."

He studied her for a moment, his hand going into his pocket before producing a flick knife. After cutting away the tape around her ankles and pulling it off she held her wrists out to him.

"No."

Shit! She'd hoped he would have a little compassion and free her hands, too, but it seemed not. At least her legs were free.

She hurried over to the bathroom, shut and locked the door, and used the facilities, before washing her hands. The only items in the bathroom were an electric hair dryer and some complimentary soap, shampoo, and conditioner. The window was too high up and too small for her to even try and attempt an escape through it. There was nothing in here that she could use as a weapon.

A fist thumped on the door. "Come out now or I'll break the door down."

Sabrina took a deep fortifying breath, unlocked and opened the door. He grabbed her arm and tugged her back over to the chair. This time, when he got the tape out, he secured her legs to the legs of the chair and once more covered her mouth.

She hoped that her men were looking for her and found her before the prick did something bad. He'd closed his laptop, and now he was staring at her like she was a piece of meat. Her heart skittered, and her skin crawled. This was definitely not good.

She lowered her eyelashes but kept watching him from beneath. She was too scared to take them off of him.

She eyed the bottle of beer he was drinking and hoped he kept right on drinking until he'd emptied the contents of the small fridge, but she knew that was wishful thinking.

All of a sudden, he placed the now-empty beer bottle on the bedside table, stood up, and stalked toward her. She shrunk back in the chair when he gave her a feral grin that didn't reach his eyes.

He pulled his knife out, squatted down, and slid it through the tape binding her legs to the chair. He gripped her upper arm hard, tugged her to her feet, and hauled her up. She tried to yank her arm out of his hold, but his hand was too big and too strong and he tightened his clasp. She whimpered in pain, but again the sound was muffled.

And then she was being dragged toward the bed.

* * * *

Trick knew as soon as Luke flicked the switch to his emergency lights off that they were getting close to their destination. "How long?" he asked.

"We should be meeting up with the deputy any second," Luke answered.

Trick saw a uniformed man step out into the road and hold up his hand. Luke slowed the car, pulled over, and they all got out. He glanced around and saw the lit sign for the motel about a hundred yards away.

"No one has come or gone from the room he's holed up in. Sheriff Snow says the only weapon he's seen on our perp was a knife."

"That doesn't mean he doesn't have more," Damon said. "This guy has been charged with assault, armed robbery, and a lot of other shit. He'll be armed and dangerous."

"So are we," the deputy replied.

"Let's go," Luke interrupted. "We have a hostage to save."

They moved quietly, staying to the shadows and out of sight of the window the deputy pointed out. Luke called Trick and his brothers over. "I want you three staying out of the way," he whispered. "None of you are armed and I don't want any of you getting killed."

Trick nodded but stared determinedly at Luke before saying, "We'll stay back unless we think you or Sabrina need our help. Have you got a rifle?"

"I don't want—" Luke started to say before Tristan cut him off.

"We're all crack shots. We used to go hunting with our dad when we were younger. One or all of us can back you up."

"We've only got two," Damon said before heading back to the car. When he came back, he had two long-range rifles with scopes and handed them over.

Tristan took one, and Trent took the other.

"Go to the far side of the parking lot and keep watch on the window and door," Luke ordered.

Damon reached behind him and pulled out a Glock. "Do you know how to use this?" he asked Trick.

"Yes."

"Good." Damon handed him the gun before he and Luke moved in.

* * * *

Sabrina trembled when the bald guy shoved her onto the bed. When he followed her down, she swore her heart stopped. He grabbed her bound wrists and shoved them up above her head before he shifted and covered her body with his. Bile rose in her throat, and she turned her head to the side. She gagged when he licked her neck and screamed when he bit into her flesh. He lifted his head and chuckled, but he hadn't lifted it high.

She didn't think. She reacted. She slammed her head forward into his face. Pain blasted through her forehead and into her brain, but she was pleased when he roared. A large hand wrapped around her throat and squeezed. She wriggled and bucked, trying to get him off of her, but it only helped him get her sleep shirt up over her hips until it was above her breasts. Tears leaked from her eyes when he ripped her panties off and then he covered her with his hard, brutal hand, his nails scratching her skin as he moved.

She twisted and turned, not willing to give in and let him rape her. She screamed when he bit down on her nipple. He was going to rape her, and there wasn't a damn thing she could do about it. He was too big and strong.

He shifted, pressing her legs further apart with his knees, and then she felt him fumbling with his jeans. Sabrina pulled inside herself and thought about her men. How it felt to be touched and loved by them, escaping from the reality of her situation.

* * * *

Trick wasn't about to stay back like Luke had ordered. Sabrina had been taken on their watch, and he was going to help get her back. He glared determinedly at Luke and was pleased when his friend didn't demand him to stay back.

They heard a man yell and a muffled scream. "Now," Luke ordered.

He moved up to the motel-room door and kicked it in, diving and rolling through the door. Damon dived and rolled to the other side, and Trick peeked around the edge of the door as Sheriff Snow stood just inside with a gun aimed at the bastard on top of Sabrina.

"Let the woman go."

Sawyer rolled from the bed, dragging Sabrina with her, his hand around her throat. Her shirt fell down to cover her nakedness, but Trick kept his eyes on the bald bastard. If he got the chance to take him out, he wasn't going to hesitate. He had a knife to his woman's throat.

"Not a chance," Sawyer growled. "You and I both know she's my only way out of here. If you don't want me to slit her throat you'll give me a clear passage to my car and will let us leave."

"Not happening," Luke snarled. "Release her."

Sawyer didn't answer but pressed the tip of the knife harder against Sabrina's neck, making a small cut, and blood dribbled out and down her skin.

Trick looked over to where Tristan and Trent were and gave them to the signal to shoot if they had a clear shot. He peeked at Luke and was pleased he had. He was telling him to back up and hide. They were going to let Sawyer bring Sabrina out. The bastard hadn't seen him, and if the four lawmen could keep him distracted, Trick could take him down from behind.

He edged back, looking for somewhere he could conceal his body, and saw the small shrub in the garden. He ducked down behind it just as the sheriffs and deputies exited, backing up until they were in the middle of the parking lot. At least they weren't obstructing Tristan's and Trent's lines of fire.

Trick heard Sabrina whimper, but he didn't look at her. He needed to keep calm and his eyes on Sawyer while he awaited an opportunity to take him down. He didn't know if she did it on purpose or not, but one of her legs pressed between Sawyer's, and they both went tumbling to the ground. The knife went flying off to the side, and since he was closest, Trick moved in.

He placed the barrel of the gun against the back of Sawyer's head, pressing hard. "Move and you're dead."

Luke, Damon, and Snow hurried over, cuffed Sawyer's arms behind his back, and dragged him off of Sabrina.

Trick knelt down beside her and pulled her into his arms. Tristan and Trick were there a second later.

"Are you okay, honey?" Trick asked as he released his hold on her and ran his hands up and down her arms and legs. He carefully removed the tape from her over her mouth and cringed when she sobbed. "Did he hurt you? Do you want me to call the paramedics?"

"No," Sabrina sobbed and then threw her bound arms over his head and around his neck and clung tightly. "I was so scared I'd never see you again. I love you all so much."

Now that she was safe again, Trick felt the adrenaline leaving his system and he started trembling. He wasn't sure who was shaking more, Sabrina or him.

"Sabrina, where did he hurt you?" Tristan asked as he cut away the tape from around her wrists. He took hold of her hand and pulled her arm from around Trick's neck.

"H–He bit me and scratched me, but that's all. I'm okay."

"Where, baby?" Trent asked in a tremulous voice.

"Uh…I'm fine. I just want to go home."

Trick released her when she reached for Trent, and his brother lifted her into his lap and held her close.

"I'm not moving until you tell me where he touched you," Trent said quietly.

"You got to me in time. It's not necessary…"

"I'm going to need a statement, Sabrina," Luke said as he squatted down next to her.

Trick saw her shiver and quickly removed his sweater before passing it over to Trent. Trent helped her put it on.

"Thank you."

Trick nodded.

"If you're not up to giving a statement now I can come by tomorrow and get it," Luke suggested.

"No. I just want to put all this behind me. Can we go sit in a car or something? I'm cold."

Trick and Tristan helped Trent to his feet since he was still holding Sabrina, and then they were heading back to Luke's car. Trent was about to get in with Sabrina, but she reached out and grabbed Tristan's shoulder.

"I need a hug from you, too, Tristan."

Trent passed her over to Tristan, who then got into the backseat of the car with Sabrina on his lap. Trick and Trent got in on either side of her, and Luke got in the front. Damon was still dealing with Sheriff Snow and his deputy.

"I'm going to record what happened if that's all right with you, Sabrina," Luke said.

Sabrina nodded, and then she began talking. The more he heard, the angrier Trick got. He wanted to get out of the car, walk over to that bastard, and put a bullet in his head. The only thing stopping him was he would end up in jail and not be with his woman.

He was so angry he wanted to go over to Sheriff's Snow's car, drag Sawyer from the back, and pummel his face to a bloody pulp. When he'd heard that bastard had bit one of Sabrina's nipples he'd nearly lost control. If she hadn't looked over to meet his eyes right then, he wasn't sure he wouldn't have lost it. The thought of that fucking bastard having his hands and mouth on her sent a red-haze of rage over his eyes. He was thankful when Tristan had grabbed his thigh and squeezed hard because he may just have ended up in jail for murder. Both Trent and Tristan had looked just as angry as he felt with their jaws clenched tight and the muscles in their jaws ticking.

Trick had had to turn away at one stage so Sabrina couldn't see the tears in his eyes. He had a hard time blinking them away, and when he looked back at his brothers he'd seen the sheen of moisture in their eyes, too. Sabrina had every reason to be in tears, but she'd kept her shit together better than he and his brothers had. She had amazing strength, and that was the only reason he'd stayed by her side and not gone after Sawyer.

By the time she'd finished giving her statement, she was yawning and could barely keep her eyes open. Damon got in, and then they were headed back to Slick Rock. Trick clung to her hand as he stared out the side window and thanked God that their woman hadn't been seriously injured, raped, or killed. He turned to watch Sabrina as her eyes slid closed and she fell asleep. Trick was going to have a hell of a time letting her out of his sight after this horrible, fearful night. It was going to take time for him to get over the fact that she had been taken while they were on watch. Guilt was a horrible emotion, and although he and his brothers hadn't left her alone and in danger on purpose, it should never have happened.

"She's safe," Tristan whispered and then kissed Sabrina's head.

Trick nodded. The knot of fear in his gut was finally beginning to dissipate and he was breathing easier.

Trick was glad that Sheriff Snow was going to keep Sawyer in the lockup overnight, and Luke was arranging for the FBI to pick him up in the morning. The agent Luke contacted told the sheriff that Sabrina wouldn't have to attend court, since the case was such a high priority. Sawyer and Noble were going to spend the rest of their lives in prison in the high-risk solitary confinement section of the most secure jail in the US and would never be released.

Trick was relieved that Sabrina would never have to see either man again and they could get on with their lives.

There was only one thing left to do.

Chapter Fourteen

Sabrina was happy to be free from fear and living on the run. It had been just over a week since Sawyer had kidnapped her, and even though she hadn't had any real injuries, she was having nightmares. She woke up in a sweat, shaking, crying, and screaming, and it was her three men who calmed her down.

She loved them so much, but they had been a little quiet since they'd been back at their house and she began to wonder if they wanted her to leave, but she didn't think so. At least she hoped not. They told her they loved her each and every day and she reciprocated, but something was wrong.

Trick had gone back to work at the bank, but according to Tristan and Trent he was working way fewer hours than he usually did. That was good, because he looked tired. Maybe the fact that she was having nightmares and waking everyone up several times a night had to do with how quiet they all were.

Rachel had dropped in to visit one afternoon and had brought a few of the other women to meet her. She had had an immediate affinity with Tori Katz, Cash Morten, and Kylie Badon and couldn't wait to meet the other women she'd been told about, but what was most important right now was finding out what was bothering her men.

She decided it was time to take the bull by the horns, and she was going to do it tonight straight after dinner. She already had the roast in the oven and the veggies prepared. All that was left to do was put them in the oven and in the steamer. She'd made apple strudel for dessert earlier in the day.

Trick was a little later than usual getting home and had just enough time to clean up before sitting down to dinner.

Tristan and Trent talked about the new project they wanted to start, but Trick remained quiet while they ate. When they were all finished with the main meal, Sabrina decided it was time to find out what the problem was.

But first she cleared the table with Tristan and Trent's help and brought over the freshly brewed pot of coffee and mugs. She sat down next to Trick and covered his hand to get his attention. "What's wrong, Trick?"

"Nothing." His hand curled into a fist beneath hers.

"Bullshit! What happened to communication being the key to a relationship?"

"Do we have a relationship?" Trick asked.

Sabrina pulled her hand back and stared at him. Her chest was aching, and it felt like her heart had just broken in two. Her first instinct was to get up and walk away, but she ignored it, took a deep breath, and released it before continuing on. "What the hell do you mean by that?"

"I thought that now you were safe you would want to move on with your life," Trick said.

Sabrina met his gaze and studied him. His body was taut with tension, but there was pain in his eyes he was trying to hide. What the fuck?

"I am moving on with my life. I've already started looking for a job."

"Yes, I know."

"Do you have a problem with me working?" she asked angrily.

"No."

"Then what's this near-silent treatment all about?"

"Have you been looking for a place to live, too?" Trick asked.

Sabrina frowned. "Why would you even ask me that? Of course I haven't."

"Then why have you been looking at the property market?"

"I haven't." She nearly yelled her answer.

"Then who did? I got home the other night and the screen was still up on the computer in the office."

"Oh, for God's sake. You stupid, stupid man. Don't you talk to your business partner?"

"What? Who?"

"Tori." Sabrina sighed with frustration. "Tori had been looking at the property market. She told me the Moms and Bubs shop is doing so well that you will either need to expand the business and split the store in two, one for the mothers and another for the babies, or you'll need to find a bigger building to fit all the new stuff you've got coming in."

"She did?" Trick asked as he sat up straighter in his chair.

"When's the last time you saw her?"

"Um…a couple of weeks. I was trying to keep you safe, and then I was busy catching up at the bank."

"She didn't contact you?"

"Uh…she left a couple of messages, but by the time I remembered to call her it was late and I put it off." Trick took a sip of coffee. "So you're not looking for a place of your own."

Sabrina got up from her chair, walked over to Trick, and straddled him before cupping his cheeks in her hands. "I love you and your brothers. You are my world. Why the hell would I want to leave?"

"You don't?"

"No."

Trick looked sheepish, and then tension eased from his body. She leaned forward and kissed him passionately. He took over, and it turned wild and hungry, and he released her after a few moments. "I'm sorry, honey. I should have come and asked you about it right away."

"Yes, you should have."

"Do you forgive me?"

"If you agree to marry me, I will."

"Did you…"

Chairs scraped, and then she was being lifted from Trick's lap by Trent and was up against his chest. "I love you, baby. Yes, I'll marry you." Her reply was cut off because he kissed her until she had no breath left in her lungs before passing her over to Tristan.

Tristan lowered her to her feet and knelt before her with his hands clasping her hips. "I love you, Sabby. I would be honored to marry you." He stood up and kissed her until her knees were weak.

She squeaked when she was scooped up, and she slung her arm around Trick's neck as he carried her down the hall to the bedrooms. He sat her on the edge of the bed and knelt down in front of her. "You are my heart, my soul, and my life, Sabrina Brown. Will you marry me?"

"Yes, you big dope."

Trick grinned, got up off his knees, and tugged her to her feet.

Her three men divested her of her clothes and then quickly shucked their own.

Tristan was naked first. He lifted her onto the bed and kissed her rapaciously. His hands cupped and kneaded her breasts and smoothed down her belly until he reached her mound. His fingers slid through her wet folds, and then he pressed one up inside of her. She moaned and gripped his hair when he kissed his way down her body. He pushed her legs apart before licking and sucking until she was on the verge of climax.

He moved up over her, and as he stared into her eyes, he thrust his hard cock into her cunt until she felt his balls against her ass, before rolling them both over until he was the one lying on his back and she was on top of him.

Trick got on the bed behind her, and after positioning her the way he wanted, he began to prepare her ass with the cool gel. She groaned when he pressed two slick fingers into her anus and tried to push further down onto Tristan, but he held her still with his hands on her hips.

By the time Trick rasped out, "She's ready," Sabrina was on fire.

Trick began to gently drive his hard cock into her ass, and Sabrina wasn't sure she'd be able to hold off coming before he got all the way inside.

She looked around the room, trying to take her mind off the pleasure of having two dicks inside her and saw Trent on his knees next to her. She reached out, grabbed his cock, and pulled it to her mouth. She licked and sucked, twirling her tongue around the broad, bulbous head, and then sucked the tip into her mouth. He groaned, she hummed, and they all began to move in sync.

Trick withdrew almost all the way from her ass, and as he stroked back in, Tristan pulled out to the tip in her pussy. With each rock of their hips, they increased the pace and depth of their sliding cocks, making the warm, glorious friction inside her build.

She bobbed up and down Trent's cock, taking as much of him as she could until he hit the back of her throat. She undulated her tongue over the sensitive underside each time she drew back, making sure she gave him as much carnal decadence as she could.

The fire simmering grew hotter and brighter. Her pussy was so wet she was dripping, and the pressure built higher and higher. She was on the precipice about to go over, but she wanted to make Trent come first.

Using her free hand, she cupped his balls and gently squeezed his precious cargo before taking him down her throat and swallowing. His cock felt like it grew warmer, and then he shouted right before it jerked as he spurted cum over the back of her tongue and down her throat. She swallowed and gulped, taking everything he had to give until he eventually withdrew and collapsed beside her.

Tristan reached between them and squeezed her clit, sending her flying.

She screamed as her internal muscles contracted in what felt like a never-ending cycle of nirvana. Cream surged from her pulsing cunt, and her whole body shook.

Trick drove into her ass once more with a yell, and then he was coming. His cock twitched and jerked as he climaxed. Just as Trent rested his head on her shoulder, Tristan stroked into her twice more and roared as he orgasmed.

Sabrina slumped down onto Tristan, her muscles weak in satiation.

She had never thought to find such a loving sanctuary when her life had been in danger, but she wouldn't change a thing if she could. She would never have wanted to miss out on finding the loves of her life.

She had so much to look forward to and couldn't wait for her new life with the three Wendall men by her side to start.

THE END

WWW.BECCAVAN-EROTICROMANCE.COM

ABOUT THE AUTHOR

My name is Becca Van. I live in Australia with my wonderful hubby of many years, as well as my two children.

I read my first romance, which I found in the school library, at the age of thirteen and haven't stopped reading them since. It is so wonderful to know that love is still alive and strong when there seems to be so much conflict in the world.

I dreamed of writing my own book one day but, unfortunately, didn't follow my dream for many years. But once I started I knew writing was what I wanted to continue doing.

I love to escape from the world and curl up with a good romance, to see how the characters unfold and conflict is dealt with. I have read many books and love all facets of the romance genre, from historical to erotic romance. I am a sucker for a happy ending.

For all titles by Becca Van, please visit
www.bookstrand.com/becca-van

Siren Publishing, Inc.
www.SirenPublishing.com

CPSIA information can be obtained at www.ICGtesting.com
Printed in the USA
BVOW04s1405310315

394112BV00019B/205/P